Unexpected
ROMANCE
COLLECTION

Betrothal to a Highwayman

♦

Not What She Seems

♦

To Win A Heart

CHRISTINE M. WALTER

© 2024 Christine M. Walter.
All rights reserved. No part of this book may be reproduced in any form or by any means without permission in writing from the publisher, Christine Walter Publishing: email qrissyw@gmail.com. The views expressed herein are the responsibility of the author. All characters in this book are fictitious, and any resemblance to actual persons, living or dead is purely coincidental.

Edited by Lynne Riffenburgh, and Lauri Schoenfeld.

Book cover design by: Sapphire Midnight Designs
Book formatting design by: Christine M. Walter

ISBN: 9798878930291

Betrothal to a Highwayman
Not What She Seems ◆ To Win A Heart

Unexpected ROMANCE COLLECTION

CHRISTINE M. WALTER

A note to the readers...

In one of my short stories within these pages, I have a delightful character who's deaf. Writing true to the style of deaf communication during the nineteenth century would've been challenging. Each home or even group had its own way of signing, and it was often "broken" and more direct. So, to allow the story to flow easier, I added all the filler words that normally wouldn't be used in communicating with sign. The English language could learn a few things about simplifying. I mean, there, their, they're? Ugh.

Sign language has come a long way over the centuries. Some good changes and some not-so-great. Being forced into change by those less understanding is never ideal. Too often, the opinions of one individual condemn thousands of lives to hardship, as happened in our world's history.

I'm a writer who thrives on happy endings, but I recognize that most stories from those who've lived centuries back didn't end well. I had to share one that did, even if it's so fictional that the events aren't closely tied to what actually happened. I'm not deaf, nor do I understand everything within the deaf community. I've learned some sign language and promptly forgot most of it due to lack of use, so I'm probably not the best person to write this story. But I did anyway because I love all walks of life—except serial killers. I hope some of y'all will like it, even if it might be too short a story.

Please spread the love of reading by helping indie authors—all authors, really—and give them a positive review on Amazon, Goodreads, or anywhere you can. Tell your friends, family members, co-workers, dog walkers, the lady behind you at the cash register, the person who backed into you in the parking lot—anyone! Just spread the word!

Happy reading!

Betrothal to a Highwayman

by
Christine M. Walter

Chapter One

1842, England
Arthur

    I kept a wary eye on the two men holding the carriage driver and footmen at gunpoint near the horses' heads. Jo Collins, the leader of our lawless group, stood at the ready and called out to those within the carriage, "Stand and deliver!"

    I shifted in my saddle, watching intently for any quick movements. *Please don't let the servants do anything foolish. We need no bloodshed tonight.*

    "No, thank you," a female voice replied.

    Collins and I shared an amused glance. The lantern inside the carriage had been extinguished the moment Collins' gunshot sounded out the warning to stop. Despite that, through the windows I could make out four dark figures.

    Collins called out again in less than inviting tones, "Stand and deliver, or suffer the consequences!"

"And what would those consequences be?" She had spit and fire, certainly, but she would get herself killed if she didn't do as demanded. Unease chilled me more than the country night air breezing along the roadside and cutting through my threadbare coat. I couldn't let harm come to anyone, or I failed at my duty. I did not relish the deception nor the risk inherent in this endeavor, but I required information. Plus the criminals needed to be caught in the act. *Where are my men? They should be here by now.*

"Ya wish me to spell it out for ya?" Collins chuckled and moved closer to the carriage. I held tighter to both my own horse's reins and those of Collins' mount. In the fortnight since I'd met Collins, he'd displayed a quick temper, which gave me reason to worry for the lady. Collins pulled the door open and turned down the step. "Out with ya." He pointed his gun inside the carriage.

Even with the aid of the full moon, her bonnet hindered my ability to distinguish her features as she exited the carriage, but her figure spoke volumes. Collins whistled appreciatively. She held her hands clasped together once she alighted from the carriage. "What do you want of us?" She spoke in haughty, confident tones, but her voice sounded young to my ears.

"Who else is in there? Out with ya!" Collins waved his gun.

"Tis only my younger sister, our governess, and my maid. And you would not wish them to exit. They would only faint at your feet."

"You think swooning females—" Collins' sentence was cut off by a quick jerk of the lady's arm. Her fist had connected with such speed and force that he fell back, landing on the ground and holding his nose. Before I could respond, she held Collins' discarded gun in her shaking hand.

My heart quickened as I dismounted. *Was the woman mad?*

She pointed the weapon at the rest of us and called out, "Drop your guns, or I'll shoot the lot of you!" Her voice was forceful, but I heard the quiver of fear. She directed the gun at the man at her feet. "I'll shoot him!"

Not wishing to get shot, I kept my distance and my mouth shut. If I were to disclose to the lady my true identity, my comrades would certainly shoot me. Either way, I needed to keep a level head.

The foolish woman is going to get herself killed! My protective instincts rose. I had to do something to keep the men calm. I glanced at the men to my right, still pointing their guns at the lady's groomsmen. How devoted to Collins were they? "Gents, keep your 'ead now and don't shoot."

* * *

Rachel

"Don't try anything foolish!" I called to the highwaymen. "I know how to use this, and I will fire if need be." I nodded toward my driver and groomsmen. "Haden, Adams, Shaw, are you hurt?"

The three men shook their heads. The injured criminal stood and growled at me, cursing me with language I'd only heard but once when I'd driven through the streets of London. He moved to his horse and pulled from the saddlebag a cloth to hold to his nose. My body froze when I realized he could as easily have pulled another weapon on me. I had no experience with this sort of thing and it was showing.

The man who'd dismounted took to his horse once again, keeping a keen eye on everyone.

"Stay where you are," I commanded, trying to keep my voice steady. My hand still smarted from the jab I'd delivered, and I shook so terribly I feared I would drop the weapon. I desperately needed each one of them to speak, so I asked the only thing that came to mind. "What are your names?"

"Ya think we're thick-headed enough to gab our names, lass?"

scoffed one of the men, turning his gun to me, and inching toward his horse. *No. Not him. The man I sought did not speak with an Irish brogue.*

The man on the horse raised his hand as if he could calm the situation through this simple gesture. "Collins, get back on yer horse. Don't do anythin' foolish. Let's leave 'er be." This man didn't sound right either.

The man called Collins spat on the ground, then growled out, "You'll pay for this."

"Collins," the man near my servant made his way to his mount, "ya want a bullet in yer 'ead? Let it go." *No. His voice wasn't a match either. Too high and smooth.*

"Where might ye have learned to hit like tha', miss?" the man on the horse asked.

"None of your business. I have asked politely for you to drop your guns. Do so now." I stepped forward, trying to prove that I wasn't afraid.

Annette murmured from within the carriage. "Rachel, *please*, be careful." Her words were soft, and the men showed no signs of having heard them.

I ignored her and took another step forward. Before I could demand anything more, the wounded man climbed onto his horse. The other two on the ground followed his example.

"No! Stay where you are!" I called, but none of them listened nor paused in their hasty exit.

The footmen hurried to my side. Adams took the gun from me. "Are you well, my lady?"

"Well enough," I grumbled, peering after the men as they disappeared into the darkness.

"I've never seen a woman strike like that," Shaw shook his head in wonder. "Your brother taught ye well."

"Yes, well, he insisted I learn," I said primly.

"More like *you* insisted he teach you," Annette contradicted from within the carriage.

"Hush, Nettie." I turned to the driver. "Haden, how long until we arrive in Newcastle?"

"Not much more than an hour, my lady." He reached inside to light the lantern once again.

"We must hurry, in case they decide to return and try again." I looked to the dark English sky. The sun had just set, and the moon was well hidden behind the clouds. "With any luck, we will meet no more ruffians—and no more summer rainstorms—to delay us." I accepted his hand into the carriage and arranged my skirts around me.

The carriage bobbed from side to side as the men took their places, then we jerked forward at a quick pace.

Miss Walmsley held her hand to her chest, still out of sorts. "I never would have believed it! How you could be so forward holding that gun, I'll never know!"

I untied my bonnet and leaned back in the seat. It might look like I was handling the situation well, but now that the danger had passed, I felt faint and weaker than a sick babe. "With great effort."

"You did well, my lady, but ya could have been killed!" my maid exclaimed.

"Thank you, Norris. Nettie, please stop whimpering. We are all alive. No need to fuss."

My sixteen-year-old sister dabbed at wet eyes. "You could have been killed, Rachel. I could not bear losing another family member—not in the same way as Papa—"

"I'm well. Nothing happened," I cut her off, cringing at her words.

"Do you think one of those men was the one who killed—"

"No." I took her gloved hand in my own and squeezed it. "No. They did not sound the same as the one who . . ." I let the words drop from my tongue. I couldn't think of the night my father had died. The heartache of it felt too recent and too raw.

"Well, we shall be safe in an hour." Miss Walmsley's frown deepened, "Though I do not know why you insist on traveling so far. Had we stayed in Darlington, we would be well settled in our beds in some blessed inn instead of fearing for our lives in the middle of the night."

"It's not that late. And it's imperative that we stay in Newcastle upon Tyne tonight." I leaned forward and shooed Annette from the seat we shared. "We will arrive at our final destination on the morrow. This will be my only chance."

"Only chance to what?" Annette asked, squeezing between the maid and the governess.

I lifted the seat in order to remove the bundle of clothing and boots from within. "I need your help, Norris."

"Yes, my lady."

I lowered the seat and sat upon it. When Annette moved to return to her seat, I stopped her and indicated for Norris to join me instead. "Now, draw the curtains. I need help changing out of my gown."

Annette and Miss Walmsley gasped. Annette grabbed my arm from across the seats. "Rachel! Inside a carriage? Surely not!"

"It must be done." I glared at both of them. "And no one will say a word of this to anyone." I turned my gaze squarely upon Miss Walmsley. "Understood?" She nodded crisply.

First, I wrapped my chest with a cloth to keep my curves from showing. It took great effort to change from the traveling dress, corset, and crinoline into trousers, waistcoat, and coat within the small confines of the crowded carriage. And all the while, my sister made clear her singular shock and disapproval. Once all the bits and pieces were donned, I folded my ringlets up from the sides of my face and pinned them under a top hat.

"Hopefully all those years of play acting in the nursery will pay off. How do I look?" I asked, tilting my head rakishly.

"You look like a lady dressed as a man," Annette replied dryly. Miss

Walmsley gazed at me in silent disapproval, her lips pursed firmly. Norris, being used to my antics, appeared supremely undisturbed. "You're too pretty to play the role of a man," Annette continued obstinately. "What is this game you're playing? What purpose will this serve?"

"Never mind that. Oh! I almost forgot." I tapped Norris for her to move aside. From the seat, I retrieved another, smaller sack. Within I found the paste and facial hair I would wear. The ghastly thing looked far from natural, but I hoped, given the dim lights and drunken men, that no one would be the wiser.

Just as I finished gluing the beard onto my face, the carriage came to a stop. At the same moment, we heard someone shout from without.

"Oh, no!" Annette squeaked.

"Not again," I groaned.

Voices called to each other, but I could not make out what was said. I held my breath, waiting for the words, "Stand and deliver." But they never came. Suddenly, Adams opened the door. "Do not fret, my lady." His eyes widened as he took in my altered appearance. "It's uh—uh—the constable. He wishes to speak to you . . ."

"Oh, heavens," I moaned, trying to calm my rapidly beating heart. "What does he want?"

"It seems he has already caught the bandits that accosted us earlier, my lady. The constables are holding them for you to identify."

"Can't *you* identify them? You saw them, too."

He shook his head. "They want your statement to convict."

"Oh, very well." I took a steady breath and turned to Annette. "You'll have to pretend to be me."

"I cannot!" she cried, scandalized.

"Well, I can't very well be myself in *this*," I waved a hand at my manly garb.

Annette threw up her hands helplessly and grumbled as she crossed over me to exit the carriage. Through the closed door, I could hear only bits and pieces of the conversation. Then she cracked the door open and leaned her head in again. "They don't believe I am you," she whispered, a smile tugging at the corners of her lips.

I pressed my own lips together and let myself out of the carriage. The number of men on horseback had doubled since earlier that evening, but now half of them were members of the law holding the highwaymen at gunpoint. "My sister does not wish to behold the miscreants again, sirs," I said, trying to mimic a man's baritone voice.

"The lady need only look out the window and confirm if these men are the outlaws that attacked her," the closest man replied.

I turned back to the carriage and instructed in low tones, "Miss Walmsley, lean over without showing your face, and pretend to look."

She did so, and I turned to address the group once again. "She confirms it—but . . ." I looked closer. Three men sat with hands tied to their mounts, but one sat upon his horse with no restraints. Neither was he grouped among the lawless. "That man there," I pointed. "He is one of the men who tried to rob my sister."

"Yes," one of the constables nodded. "He is one of us, working undercover as you might say. He helped us apprehend the miscreants."

"Then why do you need my—my sister's—help in identifying them?" I'd had enough of this. "You have your proof. Now we are tired and do not wish to be delayed any further. I bid you goodnight."

"We thank you for your time, sir," the constable nodded.

Much to my relief, we parted ways and our carriage continued unmolested. The inn at Newcastle was a welcome sight. We were taken to our rooms and our luggage was brought in. Midnight drew near, and I did not wish to waste any more time. As the others unpacked and settled in for the night, I quietly slipped out the door. Hurrying through the streets, I searched carefully for the alehouse the man I sought was rumored to frequent. At the least, it was a place rumored to harbor lowly, lawless miscreants.

My nerves were overwrought with the excitement of the night, but I had to press on. I couldn't turn back now. If my brother hadn't been thrown from his horse and killed three years ago, he would be here, performing this duty in my place. He would be the one to take vengeance on Papa's murderer. I knew he would crave justice as much as I did. As it was, the obligation fell to me.

The risk to my reputation was worth finding the man who killed my father. And when I found him, he would die.

Chapter Two

Arthur

"Pardon," I murmured as a couple moved by me within the tight confines of the inn's entryway. I tipped my beaver hat and paused briefly to bow. The gentleman politely returned the acknowledgement and continued on toward the stairs I had just descended. I found my comrade still wearing his constable's uniform, whereas I had already donned the trousers, sack coat and necktie in keeping with my nearby country abode. I slapped my hand jovially on his shoulder. "Success, Jones!"

"That it was, Atwater. You were invaluable to the arrest. I admire your zeal, and I hope you will join us again."

"Not for a while, I'm afraid. I am to be married soon." The words nearly stuck in my throat. I pushed the morbid thought away. "What did you think of the man who stood as witness for his sister?"

"Young. Pompous. Impatient," he answered shortly.

"Yes, he was that. You know, he wasn't mentioned among the travelers inside the carriage when they were held up."

"Perhaps he had ridden ahead."

"Could be," I mused thoughtfully. "Could be." Yet something didn't fit. How had the man known about my involvement? It was he who pointed me out, just as though he had been there to witness the whole affair. His appearance also struck me as incongruous, his voice and frame seemingly too young for someone with such a beard.

"It has been a long night, and I must escort our *guests* back to London," Constable Jones tipped his hat.

I headed down the street alone, in search of a draught to quench my thirst and calm my nerves. My mind dwelled upon the night's events with stubborn tenacity. Did the lady have any idea how close she had come to death this night? How could she have been so reckless? What could possibly be worth such a wanton disregard for her life and the lives of those in her keeping?

I entered the men's alehouse to find it quite full. Only two seats were left empty, and neither looked promising. I could sit beside the man at the bar who sounded like his hearing had skipped town and he wished everyone within a stone's throw to know what he was about, or I could sit beside a gentleman who looked like he wished nothing more than to be left alone—

I studied the man at the corner table as I slowly made my way through the crowded room. His loose-fitting clothing and full beard looked oddly familiar. As I drew near, he lowered his head and raised a pint to his lips.

My curiosity got the best of me, and I waved a hand at the seat opposite him. "Might I take this seat?"

He grunted.

I took that as a yes and lowered myself into the chair, removing my hat and placing it at my side. "Busy night."

"Hum."

I narrowed my eyes and studied him further. He sat far too tall and stiff to be a man relaxing with a drink in hand. The beard I deemed a fake, the hands too small and smooth to belong to one boasting much more than a few whiskers. His hat covered his eyes, but I did not miss the thin lock of dark hair hanging down the back of his neck.

I grinned. *A woman dressed as a man? Interesting.* "What brings you here this fine night?" I asked as I removed my gloves.

She held up her near-empty pint and tilted her head without a word.

"Not much for chatter, are you?" I asked. Just then a man stopped to ask if I cared for a pint. I ordered an ale and turned back to the woman. "Do you have a name?"

"It's . . . Phillips." The woman spoke in a low, quiet voice.

"Phillips. Good name. Would that be a surname?"

"Yes. If you please, I wish to keep my voice from straining."

"Sore throat, have you?"

"Yes."

I tsked, lowered my head, reached across the table, and lifted the brim of her hat enough to reveal her deep brown eyes. She blinked her thick lashes in surprise. I smiled at her. "Now what could possess a lady to dress in men's clothes? Tis not simply for refreshment, surely?"

"I . . . uh . . . you—"

I chuckled. "Don't worry. Your secret is safe with me, madam, if you'll only enlighten me as to your purpose in taking such an ill-advised risk."

She stood up as if to retreat. I took her hand in mine, not without noticing the inviting warmth of her skin. I held her hand firmly, so that she couldn't pull away without causing a scene. She turned her head back to me and whispered in a remarkably sweet voice, "How dare you touch me. Unhand me, sir."

Constraining her might be a bit brash of me, but I'd never met a lady so bold, and I had to admit, I couldn't help but hope for a bit of merriment. Something told me she was up to the challenge. "Now, is that any way to speak to your rescuer?"

"Rescuer?"

* * *

Rachel

"Please, sit." He waved with his other hand, indicating for me to resume my seat.

I paused, studying his earnest face, and felt the floor shift slightly under my feet. I lowered myself into the chair, eager for some relief and only because I was curious. It certainly had nothing to do with the way his lips turned to one side when he smiled, or the comforting, solid look of his shoulders filling out his coat, or the feel of his hand holding mine. I shook myself inwardly. "What is it you want?"

"Let me buy you another drink." Before I could protest, he waved at the man across the room and held up two fingers.

"I should go." My voice shook with worry that I could not prevent.

"But I have yet to hear your story. You would not begrudge a man some small diversion in exchange for your drink? Especially if that man might let slip to the owner of this fine establishment the nature of my drinking partner . . ."

I narrowed my eyes. "Is that a threat?"

"Does it have to be?"

The arrogant, ill-mannered brute! How dare he threaten me! "Why do you call yourself my rescuer? It seems you are more of a warden."

He laughed and shook his head. The drinks arrived at that moment. "Finish your drink and he'll take your glass."

Drink the rest? So quickly? The man stood waiting; I dared not disobey and draw attention. Keeping my head low, I quickly swallowed the last of the drink. I handed the glass over and eyed the full one in front of me with distaste.

"Well done," the man across from me nodded when the innkeeper left. "You might actually have him convinced."

I glared at him again. What a waste of good looks on a smug, arrogant man. Bubbles threatened to rise in my stomach. "You didn't answer my question," the belch escaped my lips on the last word, with a sound like a frog trying to speak. My eyes widened and I clamped my mouth shut. *What had I just done?*

He chuckled and winked, "You have yet to answer mine." He drank half his glass down, ending with a satisfied sigh.

"I'm looking for someone," I answered, hoping the frog within would not join the conversation.

"And? Who might that be?"

"I answered your first question, so now you must answer mine."

With his pint in hand, he waved at my own. "Do you not wish to taste your ale?"

"I have had some already."

He lifted a brow, as if to imply that he would not proceed until I drank. I sighed heavily and lifted the glass to my lips. He reached out and rested his fingertips firmly against the bottom of my glass, preventing me from taking just a sip. If I pulled away now, it would spill down my front. My eyes bugged as I drank more than I ever would have allowed myself. *Is he going to let me put my drink down at all?* Just as the panicked thought entered my mind, he lowered his hand, smiling wickedly. I wiped my mouth on my sleeve. *How barbaric.*

Then I let out another loud belch. My face flamed hot, and I covered my mouth with my fingertips.

"You're a natural," he winked and sat back against the wall dividing us from other men drowning in their pints. "You are right, however. I should answer your question. This isn't our first meeting this evening."

"It isn't?" Why did it take such great effort to speak those two simple words? It was as if they stuck to my tongue and tumbled about against my teeth.

"This is the third time, in fact."

"Pardon?" I stared like a witless fool.

"The first was when I witnessed your iron fist colliding with a certain highwayman. Perfect form, I might add," he smirked as my eyes widened, but continued without taking a breath. "The next was when you pointed me out among the guilty party—which I wasn't, to be clear. I was playing the part in hopes to apprehend them."

"But—"

"And finally, here we are—" he paused significantly, "in a *men's* alehouse."

I could only watch in bewilderment as he took another swig of ale. He smacked his lips and lifted his brows at me. "So, who are you looking for?"

I pressed my lips together.

"You don't wish to tell me?"

I shook my head, feeling the room move slowly around me, as if trying to catch up.

"What is your name?"

I huffed. "I do not wish to share anything at all with the likes of you. You're a snake—a deceiver. And I'll not waste any more time speaking with you." I slid to the end of the seat and stood. Again, the room swung lazily about. *Oh, dear. I think I am drunk.*

"Wait, sir!" he called after me as I tottered sideways toward the door. I glanced over my shoulder and saw him tossing a coin at the bartender. He caught up to me outside the establishment, where I clung to the wall of the building to gather my wits.

"You forgot your gloves," he said beside me.

I glanced at the gloves he held out, took them, then hurried on. A group of men parted as I rushed through them.

"It looks as though you need a hand," he pulled me by the shoulders into his side. I tried to push away but stumbled instead. He lowered his head to whisper to me, "Where to, love?"

I paused and squeezed my eyes shut. I knew I could not make heads nor tails of my way back. *Blast!* I needed his help if I were to return to my room without passing out. "This is all your fault!"

"*My* fault?" He chuckled. "Enlighten me on your way of thinking."

"You made me drink far more than I should."

"Ah, but you chose to drink in the first place. I'd wager the way you're feeling now is a credit to what you drank before I came along. It's too early yet for the effects of the second pint to kick in."

Second pint? That was the third, for I had been on my second when he found me. I groaned, wishing what he said weren't true.

"Where are you staying?"

"Why? Do you wish to torture me further?" Oh, I wished I could close my eyes as I walked. Why would the world not hold still for a moment?

"No. That would not be gentlemanly of me, now would it?"

"Gentleman, you? Ha!"

"Let me venture a guess. The Hogs and Hounds?"

I glanced sideways at him. *How did he know?*

"I guessed it. Don't worry. It's easy enough." He pulled me along, still tucked close to his side. "It's the first inn along the roadside, and it always has a room for the social elite. I'll wager by the grandness of your carriage and the number of servants that wait upon you, you are among the noble class."

"You, sir, are imp—imperminant—impertinent." My legs grew heavier the farther we walked.

"Come on, love. Not much further."

The blackguard had proved himself to be just that. A knave. A villain who preyed on helpless women—but no. That was wrong. He was wrong. I was not helpless. I was strong, as my brother had taught me to be. I could stand on my own two feet. "I'm not your love, you cretin." I shoved at his chest and swayed dangerously backward. Perhaps not. My own two feet betrayed me.

He caught me by the hand and pulled me forward. "I am curious . . . how did you hide all your wonderful curves?"

I gasped and slapped his face.

He laughed. "It's a mighty good thing you're a bit tipsy, or I might have a broken nose to match the highwayman's." He pulled me into him again and continued to walk while I protested his boldness.

The world around me moved in circles as we ascended a flight of steps inside the inn. When had we arrived?

"Pardon, miss," the scoundrel spoke to someone in the hall. "Do you know the room of the party that arrived earlier, just before midnight? This gentleman was among them, along with a lady and her maid and governess."

"That room there," a maid pointed in answer.

"Bless you," he answered and pulled me toward a door. "Is this your door?"

"Umm. Yes." From my pocket, I pulled out a key. But the doorknob would not hold still long enough for me to insert the blasted thing.

"Allow me." The highwayman-turned-secret-constable took the key from me and opened my door. From within I heard my sister gasp.

"It is I, Nettie," I said with a hiccup.

"She has returned, but she requires some assistance," the man beside me said as Annette rushed to the door.

Ah. My soft bed. At last.

Chapter Three

Arthur

    I could not delay my departure from the inn any longer if I wished to keep peace with my father, who no doubt awaited my return with some impatience—to say nothing of the bride and the wedding guests. I had hoped to catch the unnamed lady before leaving, but at eight in the morning, she had yet to emerge from her room. I had not seen much of her face due to the darkness earlier and the abominable beard later. Regretfully, I rode from Newcastle upon Tyne toward the country and home.

    The ride took less than an hour at a steady trot. My arrival was met with anxious relief by both my meddlesome parents. They made haste to inform me of the guests that had already arrived, hounding me as I hurried up the stairs to my chambers.

    "You will receive her well, though you are not happy with the arrangement," Father recited again as he followed me into my dressing room. "Her father and I have depended upon this union for many years—"

"And yet, you didn't speak of it until recently," I grumbled, removing my waistcoat.

"—and she has been prepared for it," he continued as if I hadn't spoken. "She is well accomplished. Speaks French and plays the piano. She is graceful, behaving with perfect decorum. Her father also boasted of her talent in the arts, though I have not yet seen her work. She is a lovely creature." His words were the same each time, as if scripted.

I sat down to remove my boots. "If she is so lovely, why is it that we are to meet on the day of our wedding? Do you expect me to run away at the sight of her?"

"My son, you have already had several Seasons in London to procure a wife. Our agreement was that I give you five years to find a wife on your terms, but if after that time you had not—"

"I am familiar with the agreement, Father."

"And yet you have squandered that time chasing after criminals and indulging in daring adventures," he waved his hand irritably.

"And in doing so, I have helped rid the roads of highwaymen and murderers who prey upon innocent travelers."

I saw the flash of pain in his eyes. I only wished he could understand my attempt to set things right. Father turned from me as if to leave. "I'm tired of this discussion. You will be at the chapel no later than half past ten."

I bounced my palm against the armrest of my seat. Nothing I said or did could change his mind. My future and my title were entangled in this impending marriage. I had no choice if I wished to keep my family and our home intact. "Yes, Father."

I had just enough time to bathe and dress before I must stand at the head of the chapel. With the help of my valet, I made it in time, with only a breath to spare. The bride, however, was late.

Whispers fluttered across the pews. The lady wasn't much for punctuality. Would this be a common occurrence in our future? Had she run off? Would I be spared the marriage after all? Thirty minutes passed before Father received word that the lady had at last arrived. My hope was dashed.

I focused all my attention on the bride now entering the hushed room, the woman soon to become Lady Wallington. Her ivory gown replete with lace, the ruffled sleeves resting just off her creamy shoulders—a vision! A wide sash flattered her thin waist. Masses of dark hair were piled on top of her head, which she kept lowered beneath a filmy veil that followed the same the style of Queen Victoria's recent wedding apparel. What little I could see of her face, I liked. She walked alone, a fact which stirred my compassion. Her father had not been dead a month, and she was walking alone toward a man she did not know.

Her head remained lowered, never meeting my eye. We said our vows dutifully, her voice barely above a whisper. At last she lifted her head, her eyes flashed and widened.

Hadn't I seen those eyes before? She gave an audible gasp, then quickly narrowed her eyes.

* * *

Rachel

Could a person *die* of embarrassment? I would welcome the possibility—if only my torture might end. Mr. Arthur Atwater, the first son of Viscount Wallington House, was the same fictitious highwayman I had met only last night. The situation could not be worse. I'd dressed as a man. I'd *belched*! And he had encouraged me to drink until I could not walk straight.

I wanted to cry.

Why had I not raised my head before I completed my vows? But I knew the answer before I finished the thought. My father had wished for the union, and if I had chanced a look at my husband before speaking my vows, I might have turned and run. The marriage had to happen if I were to have the freedom I needed.

I struggled to keep my voice even and my steps steady as we greeted the family members and friends who had gathered for the wedding. I smiled and nodded at the largely unfamiliar faces surrounding me, keeping my fingertips upon his elbow, but only just. My voice barely rose above a whisper as my head pounded with the excessive drinking of the night before. The celebratory wedding breakfast at Wallington House crawled on, and I could not eat a bite. Each time Mr. Atwater looked my way, I turned my head to avoid meeting his eyes.

Everyone cheered as we made our way out to the carriage at last. Annette stopped me before I reached the waiting equipage. Her eyes were filled with tears. "You won't be gone long?"

I took her hand and blinked away my own tears. "Not long, I imagine. I shall see you soon."

She nodded, then a devious smile spread across her lips. "But do *try* to like him. He is rather dashing."

I rolled my eyes. "And perfectly nefarious." I kissed her cheek and brushed a tear away when I felt Mr. Atwater's hand upon my back.

"Come, love," he said in my ear. He handed me into the carriage, and I waved to my sister and the few guests I knew. When they were out of view, I sat back and let my smile disappear.

Mr. Atwater smiled at me from across the carriage. I narrowed my eyes at him. His smile widened. We rode for thirty minutes with no words passed between us. He only grinned as if waiting for me to speak. I tried to ignore him and look out of the window.

"You are very beautiful, love."

"I'm not your love, cretin."

His eyes widened as if he'd just remembered something. He laughed with delight. "Ha! It is you! I did not recognize you until just now."

"What?" My heart pounded faster. *He hadn't recognized me?*

He moved to the seat beside me and took my hand in his. "I wondered what happened to you." He touched my cheek with his fingertips and smiled that lopsided smile. "Did you shave your beard?"

Gingerly, I extricated my hand from his. "You're impertinent."

"And you adore that about me," he teased.

"What? Of course not! I hardly know you." I moved to the other side of the carriage, facing the rear. "*You,*" *you deplorable snake,* "got me drunk last night."

He moved to my side again, sitting far too close for comfort. Why wouldn't the man leave me in peace? "And you were a good sport to go along with it," he agreed.

"You're a rake. Do you meet all your women that way, intoxicating them to the point that they can't string two thoughts together?"

"You are the only woman I've ever met in a men's alehouse." His eyes danced with amusement.

"I didn't go there on a whim, sir. I—"

"Arthur." He moved to take my hand again, but I folded my arms across my chest.

"What?"

"Call me Arthur. Not *sir.*"

I narrowed my eyes. I might just *sir* him to death. He had embarrassed me and it was his fault my head felt like it had replaced the wheels of the carriage.

He leaned closer, so that his shoulder touched mine. "What caused your delay this morning? Second thoughts?" His voice was teasing, but his eyes probed mine searchingly.

"No. I—" I touched my throbbing temple and pressed my eyes closed.

"Ah, the aftereffects. I suspect you've a headache to rival your worst." Again he reached for the hand I held at my head. I sucked in a quick breath at the sharp pain in my knuckles as I snatched it away. Then he took me by the arm and gently pulled my hand closer. "Hold still. I do not wish to hurt you." He carefully removed my glove and studied my hand closely, moving my fingers as he did so.

I winced and tried to remove my hand from his firm grasp. "Please—"

"It isn't broken, but I'd wager it's bruised from the punch you gave Collins last night," he grinned.

"Collins. Is that your friend?" I asked pointedly.

He brushed my hand lightly with his fingertips, and my body responded with a flutter that spread all the way to my limbs. *Oh! He is more handsome than he has any right to be!*

"No," he said. "I told you, I was acting, *pretending* to be a highwayman."

His gentle touch clouded my mind and warmed the interior of the carriage. I took a deep breath. "I could have been killed, and you just sat there, letting them hold guns pointing right at me."

"If Collins or the other two men had acted on their threats, I would have ended it."

"And if they were quicker?" I looked into his eyes, challenging him. *What a lovely shade of blue.*

"They would not act without good reason." Another grin spread across his face. "Would you wear trousers for me again?"

Pon rep! He's nothing but a cad! I shoved him away and moved to the other side of the carriage. He leaned over me, but his attention was suddenly drawn to the window. "Ah, we are here."

I followed his gaze, looking blankly at the long driveway before us. "Where?"

"The cottage of my mother's family. We are to stay here for a few days at least, then move on to London, where we will travel by yacht to France."

My heart quickened. I'd always wished to tour France—but I couldn't think of that now. I had an objective to complete. Finding my father's murderer before the trail ran cold was imperative. Before I forgot the sound of the man's voice. My mind wandered over the plans I had made. I didn't even realize the carriage had stopped until Mr. Atwater held his hand out to me.

"Rachel, love."

I frowned at him, pushed his hand away, and descended the steps on my own. The cozy and romantic cottage held an inviting presence about it, but I couldn't enjoy it. I couldn't stay. Mr. Atwater was only valuable as a means to my freedom. As a married woman, I could travel without escort and access my inheritance. I glanced over my shoulder at the man who followed me, my husband in name only. The sun was still high in the sky, and I wondered how I might pass the time outside of his presence. Did this cottage have a garden?

I understood the need for a cook, two maids, and a butler, but *three* footmen for such a small cottage? Add to that my own maid and driver who had followed in my coach behind us, and the cottage was quite full. I studied the bedchamber I had to share with my new husband. He stood at the window with his hands clasped behind his back. "Such a fine day. Not a cloud in sight—oh, wait. There is one," he gestured.

Norris opened my trunk. I held up a hand to stop her. "Leave it. There's no need for that," I said quickly. Mr. Atwater turned and looked questioningly at me. I swung my hands behind my back and lifted my chin. "There's no need to unpack if we are only staying a short time," I explained airily. I looked down at myself. "I only wish to change from this gown into the blue one. Everything else can remain." Norris nodded and retrieved the gown.

Mr. Atwater continued to gaze at me with raised brows.

I returned the look. "Will you not give me privacy to change, sir?"

He took a long breath, as if put out, but in the end he left the room.

I changed quickly with help from Norris, then found my way outdoors.

The garden was set just outside the house, and I had toured the entire area in the span of a few short minutes. Wishing to lengthen my time alone outdoors, I continued to walk the same path again.

"Might I join you?"

I jumped at the sound of Mr. Atwater's voice and swung around.

"Forgive me, Rachel. I did not wish to scare you." He held out his arm to me. I glanced down at it, then turned to walk on alone. He picked a flower and held it out. "For you, my dear."

"Sir, I am the daughter of an Earl. My lady will suffice."

"Ah, but you are my wife. So I may be as intimate in my speech as I see fit."

I stopped and turned to face him. "Do you delight in vexing me, sir?"

"Absolutely. I love the way your brow creases and your eyes alight with fury. Yes! Just so," his finger trailed along my brow. "You do that marvelously."

I slapped his hand away and he chuckled. I turned to stalk away, but he took hold of my hand and spun me into his arms. "Let go of me." The words that passed my lips didn't reflect the way I felt as my heart pounded in my chest.

"I think you're still upset with me on account of our first meeting."

I rolled my eyes heavily.

He released me but kept hold of my hand. "Is it that I was there amongst the thieves and ruffians to begin with? Or that I didn't immediately come to your aid, sweep you off your feet, and declare my undying love?" I huffed and rolled my eyes again, but he continued unperturbed. "Or is it that I found you out when you were trying so hard to disguise yourself?"

I lifted my chin and marched toward the house.

"Allow me to address some of your vexations." He pulled my arm to slow me, and I did, so as not to injure my wounded hand again. "First, I could not show the men that I was against them in any way. If they had found me out, they would have shot me on the spot. Just as you did not wish to be discovered in the alehouse, I did not wish my disguise to be made known. Although I doubt that room full of drunken men would have shot you. You're too much of a distraction for that."

I stopped and glared at him.

He smirked back at me, "I don't think that look has the effect you intend."

"Perhaps you were dropped on your head too often as a child to comprehend the meaning of it," I retorted.

He threw back his head and laughed deep and long. I almost cracked a smile. His laughter would undo me if I weren't careful. He took my other hand and held me in place as he continued, "Second, had I truly thought you were in urgent danger, I would have risked my life to save you."

The stiffness in my back eased a bit as I considered his declaration. "You would have?"

"Without a second thought, I would have," he answered with a gentle smile. His steady gaze stole my breath. I tried to look away, but I could not. "And as for the alehouse—"

The mention of it brought me sharply out of my stupor. I stiffened.

"I found you charming and so very intriguing that I had to learn more about you. Not only were you brave to stand up to those men on the road, but you had the fortitude to enter a room full of men likely to overwhelm you with their innumerable charms if they'd discovered who you were."

"And you didn't know who I was?"

"Not at all."

"So you flirted with me?"

"I did indeed."

"You flirted with a woman—a woman, I might add, that you didn't know was your betrothed. You flirted with a woman without so much as a thought for your future wife—the woman you were to marry the following day." I folded my arms.

His smile faltered.

"You are a rake, just as I have said."

"No. That's not—"

"When I asked you, sir, if you entertained other women in the same manner, you merely claimed I was the first you had made drunk in a *men's alehouse*. Which implies that you've caused other women to be drunk elsewhere," I raised my brows expectantly.

"That's not what I—"

"So then, how many women have you gotten foxed and taken home with you?"

Mr. Atwater spluttered and huffed. "That's not at *all* what I meant. And the answer is zero—and did you just say *foxed*?"

"Yes, I did. Isn't that the right word?"

He laughed and shook his head. "Yes, *my lady*. But how do you come to know such a word?"

"And did you just say *zero*?"

"Zero," he affirmed, his blue eyes unwavering.

I folded my arms and tilted my head, studying him doubtfully. "I find it very difficult—nay, impossible—to believe that a man of—whatever age you are—has never enjoyed the company of a woman."

"Not all men are rakes, my dear."

"That may be true, but it does not follow that *you* are not."

He lifted his brow. "Well, believe it, for it's true."

"You've never kissed a woman?"

"Ah, as to that, I cannot say I haven't." He held his hands behind his back and balanced for a moment on his toes. "But surely stealing a few kisses as a young man is not to be confused with seducing a woman."

I read the truth in his eyes as he held my hard gaze with his soft one.

He stepped closer and placed his hands on my upper arms. As he spoke, his hands moved down my back. "Would you be willing to let me steal a kiss or two?"

I stepped back, glared at him, and stalked to the house.

"That wasn't a no, was it?" he called after me.

Chapter Four

Arthur

Rachel avoided me until supper, which we took in the dining room, silently. At least *she* remained silent. I chatted on as if she hung on every word I spoke, if only to amuse her into cracking a smile.

What was it she had such a strong aversion to? Was it my looks, my manner, the way I'd behaved on the road? I had already explained that I'd never seduced a woman, so she need not be jealous. Why did she feel the need to push me away?

Afterward, we passed the evening reading in the sitting room. Separately, of course. Then without a word, she abruptly set her book aside and left the room. I took a deep breath and tried to sort out what I would say to her when I joined her for the night—which in itself might prove disastrous.

I waited long enough to allow her maid time to leave the bedchamber. Then I rose and made my way up the stairs. Disbelief washed over me as I took in the long line of linens tied to the bedpost and trailing out of sight over the windowsill. Rachel's trunk was missing, and she was nowhere to be found. I rushed to the window and peered outside.

The flower bed below showed evidence of something large having been drug through it. "Groves!" I called out as I rushed down the stairs. My butler arrived at the door at the same time I did. "My wife—Lady Wallington—has left home. Is there any word from her servant—the maid she brought with her?"

"Her maid waited in her room before she retired, but I did notice her groomsman preparing her carriage. I thought you had ordered it, my lord—"

Without another thought, I ran out the door, without so much as an outer coat or hat.

About thirty yards up the road, I spotted the groomsman climbing into his seat. He must have only just handed Rachel in and secured the trunk. I sprinted to catch up to the moving carriage.

A stitch in my side threatened to slow me down, but I pressed on, reaching for the handhold on the back of the coach. I grasped it firmly and swung myself up onto the footman's step. The driver glanced back briefly, then turned again in shock when he saw me. I nodded my head and grinned at him. In answer to his questioning look, I waved him to continue onward. I could have insisted he turn the carriage around, but if she were determined to leave me, she would do so again some other night. This way, I could see where she went and discover the reason why.

We traveled only as far as Newcastle upon Tyne, when we stopped at the same inn where she'd stayed before. Though it was summer, the drive was wet, and I cursed myself for leaving in haste without my hat. I ducked into the shadows to wait until I saw Rachel enter the inn. When her driver returned to tend the carriage, I pulled him aside and inquired as to which room he had carried her trunk. He had no knowledge of her destination or motivation for leaving me. I entered the inn and, upon recognizing the proprietor of the establishment, offered a crown in exchange for information. The good man willingly let slip that the lady had paid for just one night. I paced near the doorway, wondering whether to confront her. Just as I had decided to act, I caught sight of her descending the stairs dressed in the same ill-fitting men's clothes and false beard as before. Her attention was all on the steps before her, and she took no notice as I sidled discreetly into the alehouse.

The door closed behind her. I followed at a safe distance, back to the tavern where we had spent the infamous evening before our wedding. I waited outside for ten minutes, then quietly entered, scanning the room. The night was less busy, but just as loud with drunken men. She slouched at a far table, nearly out of view, her fingers wrapped around a pint and her eyes fixed on the back of a broad, bearded man sitting alone. I slid quietly into the seat beside her.

"Now if you loved ale that much, all you had to do was say so. There's no need for secrecy."

Her mouth opened and closed wordlessly for some moments before she finally stuttered beneath her beard, "How did—how did you find me?"

"Wasn't hard, since I was standing on the back of the carriage the whole way. Now that I know what it's like for the footman, I feel a bit more gratitude for him."

"But you—why are you here?" she hissed through her beard.

"Why are you?"

She pressed her full red lips together. I couldn't help but admire them.

I leaned in. "I have it on good authority that I can be very trustworthy, my dear."

"Shh," she continued to stare at the other man.

My head jerked back in surprise. "Did you just shush me?"

"Shh," she held her fingers to my lips and lifted her chin slightly, her brows pulled together in concentration. I resisted the temptation to kiss her fingertips and followed her line of sight.

From the corner of my mouth I whispered, "What is it?"

"Shh."

I turned to study her face. The look in her eyes was almost desperate. I took her hand under the table. If I pulled her to me, as I wished to do, I would catch the unwanted attention of a room full of men. They did not know she was a woman, and it was imperative that it stay that way. "How might I help?" My whisper was so soft she might not have heard it at all.

She turned quickly and looked into my eyes for a long moment. She opened her mouth, closed it, licked her alluring lips, then spoke, "I was there the night my father died. I can still hear his—the man's—voice in my head. If I could just hear him speak, I would know. I could identify him."

She was there that night! My heart beat hard against my ribs, then sunk. "You're here to seek your father's killer?"

She nodded once without taking her eyes from mine.

"Then I will assist you."

* * *

Rachel

My body nearly melted into him with his vow to help me. To keep from falling apart and giving myself away entirely, I clenched the glass of ale in my hand and reminded myself of where I was. My heart grew larger simply knowing he had heard and was willing to help.

"Do you think it's that man there?" Mr. Atwater—Arthur—nodded toward the man with the bushy beard.

"I think it might be. I have only a vague memory of his appearance, but his size, the beard . . ." I trailed off.

"Someone's just left that table. Let's get a closer look." Arthur removed his dinner coat and mumbled about it being ruined by the rain, then dispensed with his waistcoat as well. He tossed it under the table, then replaced his coat.

"What are you doing?" I asked.

"Can't look like a well-off gent to play this part, sweetie." He winked, stood, and held his hand out to me, seeming to forget that I was, at present, a man. I ignored his hand and stood. He nodded toward the table. "Go have a seat."

I sat with my back to the stranger, fearful he might recognize me in spite of my disguise.

Arthur sat opposite me. He leaned in and whispered, "Go along with me."

I nodded.

"It cuts up me peace what those bobbies are doin'. A highwayman can't make an honest livin' no more." He spoke loud enough to be heard a few tables over.

I couldn't help my smile at his use of an accent. He sounded like a man of the London streets. "Hum," I grunted as though I agreed, keeping my head low and focused on my nearly full drink.

He bobbed his head emphatically and continued, "All the good 'uns are disappearin' right 'n left. Where kin a bloke go to find a fella capable of handlin' a lord who's fairly flush in the pockets, eh?" He leaned in as if he had something important to say. "I overheard a gabster say there's a carriage full o' juice pullin' outta here tonight. Iffen I kin find another hand, I'll take my chance to nab me a bit o' coin. I know yer not interested and yer got the misses to tend, but—"

I jumped at the sound of a deep, raspy voice behind me. "Yer gabbin' awful loud there, gent."

My body chilled to the bone. I knew that voice. The murderer sat just an arm's reach over my shoulder. The amber liquid in my glass vibrated in my shaking hand. Arthur's brows rose ever so slightly. I nodded just as imperceptibly.

"Gent? Ha! Do I look like a gent to ye?" Arthur guffawed and slapped the table. I kept my eyes upon him and did not turn around.

"Are ye jug-bitten or do ye speak the truth?" the man asked roughly.

Arthur leaned back and looked the stranger slowly up and down, as if considering. "Are ye interested?" he asked more soberly.

"Iffen the price is right," the man replied, glancing around surreptitiously.

"The price smells fine from where I sit."

"Where they headed?"

"Leavin the Hogs and Hounds in an hour, south toward Durham. I'll know the coach."

The stranger leaned in, speaking in a low voice, "There's an old mill south of town. Ye know it?"

"I know it," Arthur acknowledged.

"Meet me there in an hour," he tapped the table once with finality.

"And yer name?" Arthur asked.

"Webb."

"Pleasure doin' business with ye, Webb. The name's Phillips."

Webb grunted and ignored the hand Arthur proffered. He strode out without a backward glance.

I let out a breath and held a hand to my mouth, my eyes suddenly filling with tears.

"Come on," Arthur urged. "We have no time to lose." I followed him out. As we walked back to the inn, he whispered hurried instructions, "I'm going to part ways with you, but I need you to do as I say. I'm going to find my worthy comrades and a horse."

"You mean the constables?" I asked, wiping my eyes.

"The very same. One of them will drive your carriage out of town. I need you to ask your groom to ready it. Then stay with your maid in your room."

"But there are windows. He'll know the carriage is empty."

"There are curtains, are there not?"

"Well, yes."

"Then draw the curtains."

"Are you sure he'll take the bait? What if—what if you are killed?"

"It's a risk I must take."

I pulled him to a stop. "But—you have a wife now."

A smile tugged at the corner of his lips. "And does that wife care what happens to her rake of a husband?"

My chest constricted. I could only nod.

"If you weren't dressed as a man, I might be tempted to steal a kiss."

The very idea flushed my cheeks and neck with heat. I smiled mischievously. His brows lifted and his eyes moved to my lips.

After a long moment, he looked away and continued, "This is where we part. Promise you'll be careful?"

"*You're* the one in danger. You should make *me* that promise."

"I promise, then. Now be on your way!" He slapped my bottom and chuckled at my shocked expression. I hurried away, blushing and wishing fervently that I was not wearing a beard and trousers.

Chapter Five

Arthur

I found Jones at home in bed. He rose quickly and gathered a few men to lend us aid. By the time I'd secured a mount, I had a plan in mind. Four constables would ride out ahead and meet us at the rendezvous point. Jones would drive the carriage at a slow pace south.

I could have cut through town and taken the fastest way out, but then I'd not be able to check on the carriage as it prepared to leave. Sure enough, the groomsman had Rachel's horses harnessed and ready. He stood at their side, checking the traces.

From the second-story window, I thought I caught a glimpse of Rachel's silhouette. I couldn't help the grin that spread across my lips.

With a weight lifted from my shoulders, and a happy anticipation of what the future might bring for us both, I urged my horse into a steady canter. Not ten minutes out of town, beyond the last of the residences of Newcastle upon Tyne, stood an old mill. Off to the side, hidden in the shadows of the trees, I spotted Webb. As I approached, I heard the click of a gun.

"It's just me," I held up my hands, gripping the sides of my horse with my knees.

His gruff voice cut through the darkness, "Iffen ye double cross me, I'll put a 'ole through yer middle."

I chuckled softly, "Then it's best I hain't plannin' to make a May game of ye." He followed me out to a narrow portion of road, beyond which my comrades in arms waited among the trees. We guided our horses around a low stone wall and a copse of oak, hiding us from view.

He sat taller. "Are ye sure the carriage is comin'?"

"I passed it on me way out. Watched them loadin' up."

We waited in silence for a time until I saw the dim light of a carriage lantern heading our way. "That's it," I spat in the grass.

"Ye follow my lead, and ye stop the horses," he commanded.

I nodded my understanding.

The moment Webb called out, I rushed to slow the horses. Jones raised his hands when the carriage brake was pulled. "I don't want no trouble."

"Get down slowly," Webb growled.

I looked about, wondering when my men might join us. How long would they wait?

* * *

Rachel

The moment I heard the call to stand and deliver, I regretted my impulse to hide away in the carriage. I thought I would have the courage to stand up to my father's killer. Now the gun I held shook in my hands, and I knew I couldn't take a man's life. I couldn't take the revenge I'd been planning for weeks.

"I said, stand and deliver!" The call came again.

I swallowed hard. Those same words, spoken by the same man, had changed my life a month ago. How could I have been so foolish as to think I could do this?

I reached a shaking hand to the latch. It amazed me that the rustle of my skirts could be heard over the pounding of my heart. My fingers wrapped around the latch. The door flew open and my body jerked forward. The gun fell from my grasp. A hand gripped my arm and jerked me from the carriage.

I screamed as the man chuckled and pulled me to him. "A temptin' armful ye are. An' yer alone."

"Let 'er go!"

Webb turned and pulled me along with him, my back pressed to his chest. Arthur sat upon his horse with his gun aimed toward us. The man rubbed his gun up and down my arm. "An' why would I do tha'?"

The look on Arthur's face filled me with remorse. "I'm sorry," I mouthed silently.

"Because I'll break your nose if you don't!" I spoke with as much venom as I could muster.

The man's body shook as he laughed. "How do ye aim to do tha', chit?"

"I broke the nose of the last highwayman who tried to rob me. I'll certainly have no qualms breaking the bones of the man who killed my father," I swallowed back a sob.

"Killed yer father, did I? When might that've been?"

"A month ago."

"Huh." His grip tightened around my waist. "Yes, ye were there, hidin' in the carriage. I remember. Too bad I had to run off so soon or I mighta' gotten acquainted with ye then." He rubbed his bushy beard against my neck as he spoke. I cringed and struggled in his arms. "But what I can't figure is why my partner 'ere has up and changed his mind 'bout the night's revelry," he waved his gun threateningly.

Betrothal to a Highwayman

"Let 'er go, Webb."

"Why not keep her? Wouldn't ye like a little fun, mate?" Webb's gravelly chuckle sent my stomach rolling.

I locked eyes with Arthur. The vengeance I had yearned for in my grief and anger seemed now like a risk I should never have taken. As I looked up at him in the dark, I wished fervently that I had never dragged us here. He was playing the part of my hero, but he might die on this senseless road. How could I live with myself then? "Please. I love him. Don't hurt him," the words slipped out of my mouth, unbidden.

Seconds before the muzzle of a gun rested against Webb's head, I felt someone's presence behind us. "Drop yer weapon, Webb."

Webb's grip on me slackened and his back stiffened. I pushed free of his arms and rushed forward. Arthur swung from the saddle and caught me in his arms. I shook with sobs of relief against his chest. He kissed my head and held me close. Webb spit threats at us as the constables secured his hands in irons.

"It's about time you showed up," Arthur grumbled at the group behind me.

"We thought you meant the other trees," one of them said, and they all joined in his laughter.

I shook my head slowly, then turned to see Webb kneeling beside the carriage. To the nearest constable I spoke, "Sir, this man killed my father. Do I have your word that he will receive the consequences of his actions?"

"Upon my honor, it will be done, my lady," the man responded with a bow.

"Come on, love. Let us go," Arthur kissed my forehead, then turned to take my hand.

I clung to his lapel to prevent him moving away. "I'm sorry, I should have stayed behind. I thought I could help, but I—"

"I understand. You had been waiting for this chance. I should have known you would not be able to stay away," he smiled ruefully. "We should get you home, my love." His gentleness filled my heart. "Jones, would you be willing to drive us south to my cottage?"

"Oh, but my maid still awaits me at the inn," I protested.

He brushed a curl from my cheek and smiled indulgently. "I'll send for her, so that you need not return there again. For if there is anything I have learned about my darling wife, it is that she must be kept far away from alehouses and pints."

* * *

Rachel

I woke in bed the next morning, with only a vague memory of how I arrived there, but I found that I liked the arm draped around me. I still wore the same clothes from the night before. My skirts tangled uncomfortably about my legs, and my stockings had worked their way to my ankles. I turned to see that Arthur still wore his shirt and trousers also, though his cravat was missing as well as his coat. His mouth hung open, and a bit of drool escaped from his parted lips.

I couldn't help the giggle that tumbled past my lips at the glorious sight of him. He turned his head, smacked his lips, then jerked awake, as if suddenly aware that I lay next to him. He looked momentarily stunned before a smile spread across his face. "Good morrow, love." He wiped at his cheek and blushed.

"Good morning," I responded, suppressing further giggles.

"You think so? You don't mind that I am at your side?"

My face felt as though I held it over burning coals. "I don't mind."

He moved his head closer, so that I could see every fleck of detail in his lovely eyes. "I dared not leave your side for fear of you running off again."

"I won't run off ever again." I gathered a dark lock of hair that hung across his forehead and brushed it back. This incredible man had risked his life for me.

He pulled me closer. "Is that a promise?"

"I promise," I smiled and placed my hand on his shoulder. "Do you want to know why I promise?"

"Enlighten me."

"It's because you helped me. You listened and you cared. And because I . . ." warmth spread through me as I realized the truth of my feelings. "I think . . . I think I'm falling in love with you."

His brows pulled together and his lips turned up ever so slightly. "Now, I seem to remember you mentioning something about that last night. I've pondered it as I held you close—"

"Arthur?"

"Yes, love?"

"Do you love me?"

His eyes turned serious and soft. "From the moment I saw you, beard and all."

I laughed and ran my fingers through his hair. "Then, Arthur?"

His eyes rolled back as he closed them. "Yes, my sweet?"

"Kiss me."

He smiled wickedly as he opened his eyes again. "Without delay, love."

His first kiss tickled my lips ever so softly, creating a stirring warmth deep within. As his lips moved with mine, becoming more urgent and filled with passion, the stirring warmth leapt into a raging fire. One thing I knew for certain as I kissed this unexpected, vexatious man, was that life would never be dull, and I would always feel safe in his arms.

Not What She Seems

by Christine M. Walter

Chapter One

Owen

Of all people to have written to me by way of post, I never would have thought of Mr. Donaldson to be that individual. I never met the man, even if we socialized within the same sphere. Evidently, his wife, the new Mrs. Donaldson, had encouraged him to write to me. Curiosity held me bound, so I skimmed through the short introduction.

I am sure, Lord Harrell, that you are wondering what could be the reason for my writing.

"Indeed, I am most curious," I said aloud and I settled deeper into the chair at my desk facing the east windows of my study.

My wife informs me that your two families were once neighbors. You may remember her as Miss Fanny Brant, though she is six years your senior.

Yes, I did remember her. Our families kept one another informed one way or another. My mother, God rest her soul, had oft spoken fondly of Fanny Brant, who married a Mr. Spears at the tender age of seventeen. I had encountered her and her late husband several times over the years, happily engaging in conversation. Since my mother's death and my father's near ruin, I had lost contact with far too many acquaintances. Deploring those last memories of my parents, I shifted my mind back to the missive.

You were but a small lad when she married her first husband, but she has never forgotten your delightful family! But I digress. I shall get to the point.

Please do.

I understand that it has been many years since your late wife's passing, and you have been alone for some time.

I cleared my throat. Three lonely years.

Why must he bring up such a topic? I continued on, reading his wife's praise of my character and his own praise of my career in Parliament. I puffed out my breath. "Get on with it." If the man knew me at all, he would know how I disdained such flattery. If I didn't know better, I would think he was buttering me up for something. Thanks to my father, most of my acquaintance tried to forget I existed. Why, pray tell, was Mr. Donaldson to be the exception?

I will not pretend I do not know of your father's gambling habits, but I implore you not to despise my bringing up the subject.

Blast. There it was. I would never be free of my father's sins.

My dear wife knew of his habits even those many years ago, and we do not fault you for the financial difficulties you have since incurred. In fact, we wish you to know we have a solution.

I stiffened. "Do you? Pray tell, what is the solution?"

My wife has a grown daughter, not yet three and twenty.

Ah. The daughter. Of course. Yet, who in their right mind would wish their daughter to be connected to someone on the very brink of ruin—even if she should inherit a title?

Sweet Nicole is much too shy for a Season in London, his letter continued, *which makes it rather difficult to secure a husband. She is a well-educated young lady, very accomplished and a capable household manager, just as her mother has taught her to be. She is also quite pretty.*

Weren't they all?

Given her extreme shyness, I have little hope of her ever marrying, despite an ample dowry. And that is where we can help you, my lord. With my new step daughters forty thousand, you may right the wrong your father so thoughtlessly placed upon you.

I shifted uncomfortably in my seat. Tempting, but could I enter a marriage of convenience yet again? Would not the young lady desire a love match? "You are proposing I marry your daughter for her money?" I asked the letter, as if it would form lips and answer.

I set the page aside and paced the room. I had indeed been considering a second marriage. I was not as young as these new lads parading about—though I did not consider myself old, either. I was simply past the age of hoping for a love union. But could I truly go through with such a mercenary plan? I had to do something to save the estate and keep my staff out of the poor house. The proposition of marriage was not altogether unwelcome. I had known all along that it would probably come down to this, a title for a fortune. Better the devil you know.

I dipped the quill in ink and scratched a reply, informing the commendable Mr. Donaldson that I would procure a marriage license, as requested, and meet the family at the chapel on the late spring morning in three weeks' time.

* * *

Nicole

The bird flapped its wings and jerked its beak as though it spoke, and my mind filled in the once-familiar sound, though I couldn't hear it now. Although I had not heard more than loud claps of sound and my own voice rumbling deep in my chest for many years now, I still remembered what some things sounded like. Getting used to near silence became easier over time, for me at least. Not for my mother. She still fretted over that long-ago illness. *If only* formed upon her lips far too often.

I placed a small handful of seeds upon the bird bath and stepped back, eager to watch the robin peck at its meal. The breeze ruffled its feathers and tugged at the ribbon holding my bonnet in place.

I had learned to read lips and body language enough to converse as needed. Yet, my world only consisted of my mother, her new husband, and the servants that came and went with the change of homes. Oh, but I could not forget the birds, the sheep, the horses and other animals that let me get close enough to observe. They, too, were my world—the best part of my tiny world.

A flash of movement caught my eye. My mother rushed toward me from the garden gate, which swung on its hinges as if she'd forced it open with great abandon. Her lips were already moving before I could begin reading them. *". . . your chambers. Today of all days, you . . . wander off. We must make haste, or you . . . be late!"*

My hands formed the words I hoped she'd see. She didn't often pay attention when I signed—especially of late. *"Mother, why make haste?"*

"We haven't the time for your questions!" She pulled me by the arm toward the house. *"Not when we . . . little time to get to the church."*

"Why are we going to church?" I signed.

She paused and looked at me long enough to allow me to read her lips. *"Today, my dear, is your wedding day, and you need to look your very best."*

I jerked my arm from her grip and waved my hands about, signing far too quickly for her limited comprehension, given the confused eyes peering back at me. *"What? Who? I cannot marry so soon! I do not even know the gentleman!"*

"Calm down, Nicole. Lord Harrell is a kind man, and besides, you cannot get out of it now. You have been engaged these three weeks, and the marriage must proceed as planned." She grabbed my arm once again and pulled.

I followed numbly, certain I'd left my body behind and only my stunned spirit trailed behind her.

Chapter Two

Owen

The lady stepped up beside me. Like the great coward I was, I had not glanced her way from the moment I heard her enter the chapel. The marriage would happen, no matter what she looked like, so why should I steal a peek?

The time came for the young lady to speak her vows, yet there was a pause. The vicar waited patiently for Nicole's response. I kept my eyes forward, not wishing to bring attention to her mishap. From behind, her mother cleared her throat.

"Ah! Yes!" The hard of hearing vicar smiled at Miss Spears beside me. "We shall skip that part, as we know you are in agreement." To my surprise, the vicar continued, although she had not spoken her vows. Never in my life had I witnessed such a lapse. Surely he would recognize his mistake and correct it. Wouldn't he? Perhaps the man had grown too old for his office. I opened my mouth to protest, but he had already reached the end of the service and was now proclaiming us man and wife.

I took a deep breath and turned to see my bride for the first time. Her rosebud lips and wide, hopeful eyes took my breath away. The blue of her eyes reminded me of the early morning sky. Her long lashes could only be seen in close proximity, matching the fair curls resting upon her neck. She was stunning. So much so that I swiftly forgot the folly of the vicar and the unspoken vows.

I smiled and lifted her hand to my lips. In that brief contact, I felt my world shift from a place of darkness of which I had not even been aware, to a place of light. My heart felt open again, as if the walls surrounding it had crumbled.

She bit her bottom lip, as if trying to hide her smile, and gazed steadfastly at her feet. How was this beauty not yet spoken for? Shyness could be overcome and overlooked, surely. She had too many good qualities for a man not to wish for her company.

There were no celebrations with friends afterward, no guests to wish us well, as the marriage had taken place in such a state of haste. We entered the carriage together after Nicole made a quick and tearful farewell to her family.

She sat at my side, our shoulders rubbing at each bounce of the carriage. The bonnet she wore hid her face from me as she peered out of the window.

"You'll love Harrell House, my dear. And as soon as we are able, I'll hire you a lady's maid. As of now, we only have a few chambermaids to ensure your comfort."

She didn't turn her head nor acknowledge my comment.

Undeterred, I continued, "Your mother tells me you are a great reader. I pride myself on my studies. I have a great love of science and find insects to be fascinating."

Again, no response. Perhaps she was not fond of insects.

"What is it that you enjoy reading, my dear?"

She neither turned her head nor spoke a word.

Was she upset? Had I imagined the connection we shared? Had I imagined her eagerness? Or did I misread the looks she cast me and the small smiles she gave me?

"Have I upset you?"

She leaned closer to the window, as if the scenery beyond were the most fascinating thing in the world. Far more fascinating than I, it seemed.

"Is my company discomforting to you, Nicole?"

She glanced my way, but only briefly. In her eyes, I saw hesitancy. No smile. No words of encouragement.

I was left to stare at her bonnet yet again as I spoke to her. Had she not the sense to behave as she ought and to speak with me? "I see. Do you wish me to leave you be?"

Her gaze remained at the window.

My heart clenched, the rejection stung. "Very well. My home is just there on the hill. We will arrive in only a moment. Once there I will leave you alone, as it seems you do not wish for my company."

* * *

Nicole

Alone. With a man. For the first time in my life, I sat beside a man without a chaperone. Not only a man, but a handsome one. In the chapel, I suddenly worried the heavens might strike me down as my mind wandered from the vicar's earnest gaze to how nicely my new husband's shoulders filled his clothing. My heart fluttered again as I remembered the softness of his lips on my hand. Judging by his smile, I supposed he had enjoyed it as well.

Each time our shoulders brushed, I felt my cheeks warm and feared he might see me blush. *Oh, dear!* What does he think of me? To my shame, I could not bring myself to look at him. Tears stung my eyes. If he were to see, would he be disappointed? In my limited experience, men did not wish for watering pots to grace their presence. Would he scold me as my own parents had each time a tear formed on my lashes?

He shifted a bit in his seat, and I turned my head to chance a glance at him. He stared at me intensely. I turned swiftly back to the window. What had I done wrong? Did he find me plain? Was he already regretting the marriage? Had he seen my tears?

A large manor house came into view. My mother had said that Lord Harrell was the earl of a grand estate. Harrell House would be my home.

Lord and Lady Harrell. That was us. Yet . . . I did not know his given name. What did his mother call him? I had no way of asking until I had a quill in hand. Hopefully, once we'd settled in, I could sit with him and we could write our questions to one another. I wanted nothing more than to learn everything there was to know about my new husband.

The memory of his kiss on my hand returned to me and warmed my heart. Did I dare reach out and touch his hand? Would he receive my gesture with gladness?

The carriage stopped, and I waited until Lord Harrell exited before moving to follow. Without meeting my eye, he handed me down. My husband turned, stared straight ahead, and guided me to the house. Once inside, he turned to me. I caught the last part of what he spoke by watching his lips. I understood enough to know that the woman who stood off to the side would show me to my chambers and a meal would be brought up for me.

Are we not to dine together?

He turned and walked swiftly away. The woman said something then, but her tight lips and the small movements of her mouth made it difficult for me to understand. She turned and walked up the stairs as if I were meant to follow. She led me to a grand bedchamber with high ceilings of sky blue. The marble carvings surrounding the fireplace depicted unclothed people dancing among grapevines. The posts of the bed rose broad and tall, holding a canopy overhead. Tall, arched windows filled the room with glorious light. I smiled and turned about, gazing in wonder at the beauty around me.

When at last I returned my attention to the woman, she was glaring at me. *Dear me.* I must have missed something she said. I studied her face for any indication of what she needed from me. She nodded curtly at the maid who had followed us in and spoke through tight lips. Then she swept out the door, leaving the maid behind. I kept a close eye on the maid as she moved about the room, unpacking my things, so I would not miss her words.

To my relief, she only asked short questions requiring a nod or a shake of my head. Soon her work was done, and I was left alone.

The evening meal came and went with no word of where my husband might be. The food tasted far better than anything I'd eaten at my mother's house. After darkness fell, a chambermaid came to stoke the fire and help me into my nightgown.

With nervous flutterings, I waited upon my bed, wondering when my husband would come. My mother had told me what was expected of me upon our wedding night, the idea of which both horrified and thrilled me at the same time.

But he never came.

* * *

Owen

I'd been a married man for three days. I had only encountered my wife once in that time, and that by accident. Coming upon her unexpectedly early one morning in the breakfast room, I inquired if there was anything she needed. She merely shook her head waved her hand in an odd fashion, and I returned to my study.

Not What She Seems

I judged from the reports of my housekeeper and the chambermaids that she had no interest in running the house. She appeared even too shy to answer the maids, leading us all to conclude that she desired to be left alone.

Did she find me repulsive? Did she fear me? Or perhaps she resented the marriage? Perhaps her mother had led me to believe she wished for the union when she truly did not.

The thought of her weighed heavily on my mind as I crossed the path leading to my favorite portion of the garden. The sound of a page turning brought my head up and slowed my steps. In the shade of a willow, Nicole crouched on her knees, leaning forward as if to study something small on the ground. A book lay open on the grass beside her, and as I watched, she turned her eyes upon it, her finger running swiftly across the page.

"Good afternoon, Nicole."

She didn't look up.

"What is it that fascinates you to the point you'll soil your new gown?"

She didn't respond, but shifted to keep her back to me.

"Again with the childish ways? Will you not speak to me, Nicole? I am your husband, after all."

Not a whisper or a turn of the head. She went about her study as if I didn't exist.

"What is it that repels you so? Will you give me no chance?"

Nothing.

I stood there with shaking hands balled into fists. My heart smarted at her rejection. How could I have been such a fool as to think this marriage was a good idea?

She glanced up, a look of surprise flashing across her face, then turned to face me fully with creased brows, as if questioning why I was still standing there, irritating her. "Be it as it may." I turned and stalked away, determined not to bother her again.

* * *

Nicole

The book of insects I'd found in the library indicated that the bug before me was none other than a rose chafer beetle. The poor thing had lost a leg. According to the book, it liked flowers, and if I were to guess, it had been enjoying the nearby rose bush before its leg was so tragically severed, by what? Only the bug could know. Perhaps he'd had a near miss with a bird.

I noticed something from the corner of my eye and turned to discover Lord Harrell on the path. He looked closely at me and the book. My brows pulled together. Was he upset that I had brought the book outdoors? The sudden hatred I felt in his curled fists and steadfast glare was like a slap to the face. What had I done so terribly wrong?

Before I could sign, he turned on his heel and hastened away as if he wished nothing to do with me. My heart fell to the soft earth below.

Questions flew through my head, and sorrow at my inability to communicate weighed heavily on me. I felt again my long-sought-after wish to sink into the ground and disappear. How could I go on living like this? No one had tried to learn to communicate with me. I'd tried signing once with my maid, but she only looked at me as though I had no brain at all.

I shed tears under the tree until the shade stretched away from me and the sun hung low. I'd soiled my dress not only with the dirt and grass, but also with my tears. I must look a sight.

I retired to my room and pulled the cord I knew would summon the maid. She helped me change into my nightgown and left with the promise of supper. While I waited, I wrote a note to Lord Harrell. When the maid returned, I folded it, wrote his name on the front, and gave it to her. She tilted her head at me as though waiting for me to tell her what to do with it. I signed for her to give it to him.

Again, she looked at me with questioning eyes, then left the room. Were they really unwilling to accept me? Were they so unwilling to try to learn?

Chapter Three

Owen

A knock sounded at the door. "Enter," I called.

A maid entered timidly and curtsied. "My lord, Lady Harrell wishes you to have this." She held a missive out to me.

"Does she now?" I huffed and walked to the door to take the letter.

"My lord?" she asked hesitantly.

"Yes, Beth?" I lifted my brows impatiently.

"Does Lady Harrell . . ."

"Yes?"

"Nevermind, your lordship." I tossed the letter aside and readied myself for bed, wearing nothing but my nightshirt. I'd meant to rest my head on the pillow without reading the note, but after a few paces around the room, I gave in and unfolded the small sheet of paper.

Dearest Lord Harrell,
I wish to apologize for my failures. I know I have burdened you with

them, and that thought grieves me. Please forgive me and my weaknesses. Also, I promise I shall not take a book out into the gardens again. If you would, please, I do not always wish to be ignored.

Yours,
Nicole

Did she think my displeasure stemmed only from her taking a book into the garden? Half the books in my library had spent their day in the sun. And for her to accuse me of ignoring her! Why, she was the one administering the cut direct!

I fumed and paced the room once again. She had already heard me stomping about, so I felt not the slightest anxiety in disturbing her further. I entered her room through the door that connected ours. She was sitting at the edge of her bed and jumped at the sight of me. Her blue eyes widened when she took in my lack of clothing.

I tried to ignore the alluring nightgown she wore, her long blond curls hanging loosely over her shoulders. Instead, I tossed the note onto the bed. "How dare you accuse me of ignoring you! I have done all I can to engage you, and you've not said one word to me during the course of this *marriage*!" I could not help the bitterness of the last word.

She tumbled back on the bed with a look of shock and terror on her face. Shaking her head frantically and gesturing with her hands in strange ways, she hurried to the writing desk and dipped the quill.

"I don't need any more of your letters. I need you to speak to me!" I shouted. "Look at me when I talk to you!" I slapped my hand on the desk and she jumped. She stumbled backward and looked at me as though I would strike her.

I stiffened and looked down at the words she had hastily written.
I cannot understand when you speak so quickly.
"What do you mean you cannot understand me?" I demanded.
She moved hesitantly to the desk, watching me as if I would pounce.

She swiftly wrote another line, and I bent down to read.

I read lips well enough, but only when spoken slowly.

Understanding dawned, and I felt my stomach sink. "You—cannot—hear?"

Her brows pulled together before she wrote again.

My mother did not tell you?

I swallowed hard. "I have been deceived."

Her eyes grew big. She waved her hands about and her facial expressions showed the variety of emotions moving through her. Tears filled her eyes as she paced back and forth. It seemed she, too, had been deceived by her mother, and she looked as angry as I felt.

How could her mother and stepfather be so cruel? Never a word was spoken of her affliction.

She moved again to the desk and wrote.

What will you do? Am I to be sent back to my mother?

I narrowed my eyes. Her body trembled. The one thing I knew was that this was most assuredly not her fault, and she did not deserve to be pushed aside. "No. You are my wife."

Her shoulders lowered as if a weight had been removed. She wrote on the paper again.

What is your name?

My heart sank further. "You have married me, and you do not even know my name?"

She shook her head and frowned.

Had Nicole believed all along that I knew she was incapable of hearing? That certainly cast me in a less favorable light. In her eyes, I'd treated her indifferently. Cruelly, even.

"Oh, you poor thing." I reached out to take her hand. She stiffened as though she thought I was still angry and would harm her. Carefully, I took her hand and kissed it, holding it to my chest. "I am truly sorry."

She burst into silent tears, then pointed again at the question she had written.

I dipped the quill in the ink and wrote.

Owen Knowles.

She moved her fingers as though she were telling me something. "Are you speaking with your hands? I've heard of that, but I've not seen it done before."

She nodded. She wrote quickly, blinking back tears. A single teardrop fell upon the paper, smearing the ink. My heart broke further for her.

If it is agreeable to you, I can teach you how to talk as I do. I shall sign your name.

She moved her fingers as if she were spelling each letter. I copied what she did. She smiled and wiped at her tears. Her beautiful smile undid me, and I pulled her into an embrace. She stiffened only a moment, then lightly placed her hands at my sides. "My apologies, my dear," I said, then remembered that she could not hear me say the words. I leaned away to let her see me speak. "My apologies, my sweet Nicole. I did not know, and I am grieved at my behavior toward you."

* * *

Nicole

My heart leaped and I felt lighter on my feet. He was sorry. He didn't hate me. Oh, I thought he'd known! How could my mother trick him thus?

The arms that held me were warm and comforting. Comfort. Something I had not felt for some time now. My heart spread open and some part of him entered, as if the two of us had been waiting for one another's spirits all our lives.

Owen stepped away, dropping his hands to my own and holding them fast. I smiled at him again, then sat down in the chair before the desk.

Do you have many horses here?

I pushed the parchment over to him to read. He smiled and nodded. "Many horses. I breed them. Do you wish to ride?"

I clapped my hands once and nodded enthusiastically. I could tell he laughed by the way his shoulders shook. He held up a hand, as if indicating for me to wait. He left my side, then returned with a chair by the fire to sit beside me.

"What is your favorite thing to study?" he asked.

I love animals. But I recently found a book in your library about insects, and I have discovered how fascinating they are. I hope you are not cross with me that I took the book out into the gardens earlier. I promise not to—

He had been watching the words appear upon the page as I wrote them, so when he placed his finger under my chin and lifted my eyes to his, I wondered if he would be cross at the reminder of the book.

"I am not cross with you, my dear. I've taken that same book out into the garden on many occasions. Insects have always been *my* favorite subject."

I used signs to tell him I was relieved and happy for our common interests, then wrote down the words I used. We continued that way for hours, my writing and teaching him to sign, while he asked questions. He seemed eager to learn my way of talking, a fact which filled my heart with joy. We learned a lot about each other as the time passed, and I found we had much in common. It wasn't until the sunrise outside began to light the room that I realized we'd conversed throughout the night, never tiring.

He placed his hand on mine and brushed his thumb over my knuckles. "I think it would be a grand idea if you were to teach the servants here. Teach us all so we might converse easily with you. Would you teach us?"

Not What She Seems

I nodded with a smile so big it hurt my cheeks. I held up a hand for him to wait, then wrote upon the paper, indicating I had something for him. Next, I crouched at the side of my bed and reached underneath. The room was still too dark and the object I sought too far back, so I laid on my stomach with my feet sticking out from under the bed. *He must think me positively wild. I must look a sight with my bare legs kicking about as I scoot around. I'm acting as a heathen!*

My hand hit the object of my desire, so I pulled the box out and scooted backward, pushing my nightgown up my legs. By the time I had righted myself, my cheeks felt flushed and I dared not look at his face. *Oh! I should not have done that!*

I sat beside him once again, still avoiding his eyes. I opened the music box and lifted it to my ear. I could hear only the slightest sound, but it was heavenly to my ears.

He placed a hand on my arm to get my attention. I looked at his quizzical face. "Can you hear that?" He pointed at the box.

I nodded, then wrote. *I can hear loud noises and sounds right beside my ear. I can hear my own voice.*

"Fascinating," he said.

Forgive me for behaving as a heathen while I retrieved this box.

His face went red and then he did something I'd not yet seen him do: he grinned mischievously. "I did not mind in the least."

My face instantly warmed, and I bit my lip to keep from smiling wide. From the box, wrapped in a handkerchief, I found the object I wished to give him. I took his hand, palm up, noticing as I did that the touch of his skin warmed me further. The pocket watch slid from the handkerchief and landed in his open hand. I wrote as quickly as I could to explain.

Years ago, I dreamed of becoming a wife. My mother took me shopping, and I came upon this watch. I knew if I bought the watch, I would one day give it to my husband. I hope you like it.

Owen read the words and opened the watch. With a smile, he took my hand and kissed it. "My Nicole. I will cherish it always."

My eyes blurred with tears.

He brushed at my cheek with his finger. "I think . . . I think, my dear, you could very easily cause me to fall in love with you."

My heart leapt. I leaned in and kissed his lips once, then pulled back just as quickly. I covered my mouth with my hands, embarrassed by my boldness. His eyes were at first stunned, then his perfect lips grew into a wide smile. In the next instant, he stood, pulled me up off my chair, and spun me around in his arms. I threw my arms back and laughed. I could probably count on one hand the times I remembered laughing aloud. This laugh was one of pure joy and came unhindered.

Could he truly one day love me?

He lowered me to the floor abruptly and looked at me, stunned and smiling. "Your laugh is glorious!" He pulled me against him, cradling my head in his hands. "*You* are glorious." His eyes dropped to my lips, and I closed my eyes as his soft lips gently moved against my own. I could hear myself make a noise—what it sounded like to him I did not know. His lips formed a smile against my own. I dared not move a muscle. The warmth of his lips pressed once more against my mouth. First, the kisses were tender, then they became more spirited.

Before I was ready for it to end, he pulled away and smiled at me. I signed to him. His brows pulled together as if in question. "Did that mean, I love you?"

I nodded and signed it again. My laughter rang in my ears as he lifted me again to spin me about.

***

Two years later
Owen

My ears perked up at the sound floating down the corridor. It wasn't an unfamiliar sound, but one I didn't hear often due to her quiet nature. I rose from my desk and hurried to the drawing room. If Nicole was making that sound, then I wanted to be part of it.

My grin grew the instant I entered the room. The grand sight of my wife rolling about the floor with our two-year-old son filled me with laughter of my own. Upon seeing me, both Nicole's and Joseph's laughter increased in volume. I joined in, grabbing both and growling at my son.

Joseph wiggled away. "Oh, no! Monsser! Monsser!"

I growled and tried to grab at him. When he ran too far to reach, I turned my attention to Nicole and tickled her. She wriggled beside me and laughed. Joseph jumped and shouted, "Mama! Mama! I save you!"

The feel of her under my arm and chest turned my desire for laughter into something more intimate. I grinned at her wickedly and kissed her sweet lips. She sighed as she did each time we kissed. *Oh, how I love that sound!*

Joseph bent down, tucking his little face between us. "Monsser got Mama?"

"Monster got Mama." I chuckled and rubbed his head, mussing his hair further. I sat up, allowing my wife to do the same.

"*I have some news,*" Nicole signed, her eyes dancing with mischief.

"*And what is that, my love?*" I signed in return.

"*We shall have another little one running about the house and interrupting our kisses soon.*"

I laughed and pulled her to her feet. "It's about blessed time."

She laughed again and threw her arms around me. In her own voice, she spoke the words I loved to hear. "I love you." They weren't perfectly pronounced, but they were perfect to me. *She* was perfect to me.

"And I love you, my Nicole."

Not What She Seems

To Win a Heart

by Christine M. Walter

Chapter One

Ben

A nudge at my shoulder brought me back to reality from the adventurous world I'd created in my mind. The hero slaying the rampaging trolls would have to wait. I mentally set the story aside and turned to my blue-eyed sister. "My apologies. Might you repeat that?"

"Who are you pondering, Ben? Someone with dark lashes, or perhaps bouncy blonde curls?" Daisy grinned as if she had me figured out.

I laughed. "Nothing of the sort. You know I've only just arrived from Oxford and have not the time for such things."

"Yes, but that does not discount your having a chance meeting with a lovely young maiden along the way," she trilled, eyes gleaming.

I shook my head and gently guided Daisy to the side, avoiding a couple heading our way along the path in Hyde Park. I nodded and tipped my hat at the same time as the gentleman passing, saying quietly as I did so, "You are entirely too romantic, dear sister."

To Win a Heart

"And yet, I am no equal to my terribly romantic brother," she persisted. I gave her a sideways glance. If she wished a verbal jousting, I just might oblige her this once. "I've read some of the stories you failed to hide away," she added primly. I stopped, my mouth agape. She held up her hand. "Now before you get upset, I wish to praise you. I am impressed."

I studied her skeptically.

"Truly. You are a fine writer, and you know a thing or two about *some* romantic hearts."

"Oh?"

She tilted her head to the side. "You lack insight into a woman's heart."

"Given that I am *not* a woman, that must come as no surprise," I said dryly.

"I think it will improve when you find a lady to cherish." She patted my arm, tugging me onward.

"Oh, lud. And is that not why we are here in London?" I asked with a groan.

"Of course! We are now both thrown into the marriage mart. You for the first time and I for the third." She strove to keep her voice light, but I heard the strain and read the unease in her eyes.

"You sound worried."

"Only worried about what people will say if I do not find someone this go around. At least I'm not alone. Aurora is here too. This is her third Season as well."

"How is your mysterious friend whom I have yet to meet?"

"You'll meet her soon enough, and her younger sister, too. We are to dine with the family tomorrow, and I shall introduce you."

She paused, and as she had hold of my arm, I stopped along with her. "I ask you, brother, to be kind. She has had a most difficult year."

A young lass selling pansies by the roadside called out to us. "Buy some flowers fer yer sweetheart, gov'nuh?" The young girl looked hopefully at me. The dirt caking her skin looked to have been there a while.

I laughed. "I think my sister would rather I not call her that, but I will wager she'd enjoy a fine flower or two."

"Tha' she would," the girl answered, her cheeks reddening.

With a flourish and a wink, I produced a penny.

"Tis only a ha'penny, gov'nuh."

"Then the second bundle I shall give to my sweetheart."

"Ben?" Daisy placed her hand on her hip. "Have you been hiding something from me?"

I grinned at her and shook my head. "You know all my secrets, sis."

The lass handed over the two bundles. I gave one to Daisy, then bent down next to the girl, who couldn't be more than eight. "For you, my sweetheart," I winked again.

"Tare an' hounds! Yer a right charmer, ye are." She looked at Daisy and pointed her thumb at me. "Betta keep yer eye on 'im."

Daisy laughed. "Oh, I am well aware of that." She pulled me by the arm, but not before I winked at the girl again. "You probably made her day. You certainly gave her something to boast about among her fellow urchins."

"I consider it the greatest kindness to offer a smile to everyone, regardless of their station in life."

She patted my arm. "You have a good heart."

"Well. I have fooled you, at least." I winked. "You were saying something about Miss Wakefield?"

"Oh, yes." Her laughter vanished. "I fear for her. Last Season she was so full of life and hope."

"And this Season?"

"She is not the same, and I cannot divine the cause. When I press her for insight, she invariably changes the subject. She does not wish to be in London at all."

"That is not unusual. *I* do not wish to be here—except for the honor of your company, of course." I tipped my hat gallantly, but she only smiled wanly.

"You should have seen her excitement last year. She longed to find a husband. And this year . . ."

"This year?" I prompted.

"She has vowed never to marry. She tells me she is to die an old spinster! She has already refused one offer and turns her back on those who wish to stand up with her at the balls. It is disgraceful, but she only attends at the insistence of her mama."

"Why the change? Has her family fallen on hard times with no hope of recovery?"

"On that score, I know they are perfectly well. Her dowry is more than my own."

"Then why the sudden egress for the nunnery?" I raised my eyebrows.

"Truly, I do not know." She bit her lip and looked at me. "And there is something more."

"Yes?"

"She no longer takes her usual long walks nor rides her horse. She does not get outside at all. On my last visit, I found her spending all her time indoors, sedentary and alone."

"Does she prefer to read, perhaps?"

"It was never her favorite pastime before. She loved to dance, walk, ride, swim—"

"Swim?" My eyes widened.

"Well, yes. We both enjoy a good swim now and then. And don't look so shocked. You and I used to swim the pond as children. She is no different."

"Perhaps she has changed. Perhaps she does not wish to participate in such childish pursuits now that she is grown."

"You do not know her as I do. It is not like her. She has always been a lively, enthusiastic person. No, something has happened, I am sure of it." She sighed and looked away.

I patted her hand reassuringly. "If you are so dear to one another, I suspect she will confide in you soon. You must just be patient."

"I do not know. She is so very much reserved, yet there is a yearning and a sadness in her eyes."

"Do you think she has fallen in love with someone she ought not to have?" I asked cautiously.

"Oh no! In fact, I asked her that very question, being much afraid of the answer, and she so adamantly denied it that I cannot believe otherwise."

"A mystery indeed. What can it be that makes her so heavy-hearted?" We turned to the busier portion of Hyde Park and I braced myself for the onslaught of introductions.

"Her sister did mention an accident not long after our second Season. I don't know the particulars, but I believe she has fully recovered."

"What kind of accident?"

"Turned carriage, I believe."

"Perhaps she blames men for the accident and vows never to forgive another man as long as she lives." As soon as I voiced the words, I heard how utterly ridiculous they sounded. My sister scoffed, agreeing with my inward assessment.

Up ahead, a girl screeched. I quickened my pace as I watched a man pull at the street urchin's arm, a girl of no more than twelve. She cursed up a storm, kicking and struggling. The man was not dressed finely enough to be called a gentleman, and I wondered suspiciously at his intentions.

To Win a Heart

"I say! Unhand her!" I called loudly, striding closer and leaving Daisy at a safe distance.

"This has nuffin' to do wif you, bloke," the man hissed through a mouth full of missing teeth. "Do like the others and turn a cheek."

"I will not ignore someone in need, *bloke*. Now unhand her, or I shall land you a facer," I replied coolly.

He sized me up and glanced warily at the small crowd that had gathered. At last, he dropped the girl's arm, but not without a fierce warning look. Then he sauntered off as if he owned the park and hadn't a care in the world.

I approached the girl slowly and bent to speak to her. "What is your name?"

"Ipsy."

"Ipsy? Is that a name?" I asked in some surprise.

She narrowed her eyes at me. "O' course it is."

"Ah, yes, of course," I nodded. "Well, and what did that unsavory fellow want with you?"

"Iffin I have to spell it out fer ya, mister, then yer not all that smart. Us urchins don't last long for a reason."

I paused, taken aback by her candor—and her audacity. "It happens that I have need of a scullery maid," I said at last. "You wouldn't happen to know of anyone interested in such work, would you?"

Her eyes widened. "At a big, fine house?"

I nodded.

"I 'appen to know someone." She pointed at herself with her thumb.

"Wonderful." I gave her my card. "Present this at the servants' door and tell them I sent you. I'll be along soon to explain *iffin* they give you any trouble." I gave her directions to my home and held my arm out to Daisy once again.

Ipsy took the card, gave a quick salute, and ran off with a bounce in her step.

"Without fail," Daisy said with a shake of her head.

"What is without fail?"

"You shall never resist lending a hand to those in need. For that, I am proud to call you my brother. Yet, let us hope this one does not turn out like all your other endeavors."

* * *

Aurora

If ever someone were in need of salvation, it was I. My mother was going to do me in if I were forced to endure her presence much longer. But therein lay the dilemma. To extract myself from my mother's daily presence, I must wed . . . and that would *never* happen.

"If only I did not have such stubborn children," Mother repeated. Indeed, I had lost count of the number of times I had heard the phrase.

"Mother, I shall not be moved."

She sat beside me in the extra chair before the writing desk and took my hand, causing a blot of ink to stain my letter. "Only think of what you are giving up!" she persisted.

I sighed heavily, pulled away my hand, and crumpled the letter impatiently. "Nothing I shall miss." The heaviness of that falsehood pressed upon me.

"But you *must* marry! You cannot afford not to." The creases at the edge of her blue eyes deepened as she narrowed them at me. "If you do not agree to Mr. Waterman's imminent proposal, I shall disown you."

My eyes bugged, but just as quickly my shoulders shifted back and my chin raised. I'd been bullied long enough, and I could not simply shrink away like a weak lamb any more. This was my future, not hers. Too many years of her threats and abuse—I must do something. "Save me the bother and disown me now." I flinched at my own words. I never used to be like this.

Her abrupt slap stung, bringing tears to my eyes. It had been at least a year since she'd reacted so harshly, and I had hoped the change was a lasting one. Evidently not. Her eyes blazed, sending a surge of indignation through me.

"Aurora! How can you be so unfeeling?"

"You know the reason perfectly well, Mother! My life has changed, and I cannot look to the future as I once did. You must see that now!" My shout surprised even myself.

"Yes," her voice turned low and tears formed in her eyes. "I know. I do."

Guilt pierced my heart, yet I must stand strong. Too often she used the same tactic to get what she wished. "So I shall not marry, and if asked, I will decline."

Something flashed in her eyes and her lips thinned into a hard line. "Then you leave me no choice." Mother stood and walked to the door. "You will be at dinner tonight. Your dear Daisy Wild will be expecting you."

I nodded once. "I will be there."

"And if Mr. Waterman finds a moment to speak with you, I do hope you will at least listen to him."

I cringed. Please, not Mr. Waterman. Something in the man's eyes each time I had to converse with him made me ill and wishing I had an ocean to separate us. The very idea of entertaining an offer from him—or his merely opening his rancid mouth—caused my stomach to churn. I did not answer. I watched her leave the library with her head held high.

The clock chimed, reminding me that the time had come to dress for dinner. I grumbled to myself. Mother had taken up all the time I had to write my letter.

I stood, keeping a firm grip on the writing desk, and wished, not for the first time, that I could make use of a cane. Yet the idea of carrying such a thing was humiliating, and it would certainly draw attention.

I made my slow way upstairs to my room and pulled the bell cord. Mary rushed in. The girl never went anywhere without flying about, though I was always reminding her to slow down.

She pulled a gown from the closet and laid it hastily on the bed. I frowned. "I do not wish to wear that one."

"Your mother thought ya might say tha', but I am instructed to tell ya that ya have no choice—" she held up her hand to stop my protesting. "I'm sorry, miss. Orders are orders."

The gown had no faults. In fact, it was the favorite of all my gowns, but it looked too well with my auburn hair and blue eyes. The delicate lace layer over top of the green silk, along with the low cut of the neckline, was sure to turn a man's eye, something I wished never to do again.

I dropped the shoe I held so I wouldn't be tempted to throw it. I had half a mind to stomp into my mother's room and demand to know what scheme she would force upon me, but I knew where I got my stubbornness. She would not relent.

"You win this go around, Mother," I huffed, allowing Mary to help me into the dress. I found that even in the styling of my own hair, I had no choice. Mary followed specific instructions on how to make me appear fashionable and pretty. If not for the dismal future I faced, I would have approved and even looked forward with anticipation to the coming evening. After all, my dearest friend and her brother! If only things had turned out differently.

Now I could only make my way to the drawing room with a heavy heart.

The guests began to arrive while I remained rooted to the corner of the drawing room, where I watched families and distinguished members of the *ton* arrive. Most I had met previously, and those more polite made the effort to greet me. At last I spotted Daisy on the arm of a young man I could only assume was her brother. She saw me and pulled her brother eagerly toward me.

"Good evening, dear friend!" she breathed, taking my hand warmly in hers.

"And to you, Daisy," I replied stiffly.

Her smile faltered, but only for a moment, and then she stepped back to make way for the gentleman beside her. "May I introduce my brother, Mr. Benjamin Wild. Ben, this is my dear friend, Miss Aurora Wakefield."

I curtsied and nodded politely, trying not to stare at the handsome face before me. Daisy had never mentioned what a dashing brother she had. How very impolite. Not that it mattered. He would be kept at arm's length like the rest of them.

"It is a pleasure, Miss Wakefield." He took my hand in his and bent over it, his eyes never leaving mine. A warmth moved through my gloved hand and up my arm. When at last he let go, he straightened and turned to Daisy, his eyebrows raised. "I must rebuke you, dear sister. For I have heard you speak of Miss Wakefield often, yet never once have you let slip a word of her exquisite beauty," he said in mock solemnity.

The heat moved to my face.

"Indeed I have!" Daisy protested with fire in her eyes. She turned to me. "Do not listen to a word, Aurora. My brother fibs. Often."

Mr. Wild pulled a long face. "When have I ever so much as exaggerated the quantity of mud on my boots, dear sister?"

Daisy cut him a sharp sideways glance, but I saw the corners of her mouth twitch. "Stop this nonsense or I shall throw my glove down before you," she threatened, tossing her blonde curls.

To Win a Heart

Mr. Wild laughed and I found myself joining in.

"I must intrude before any unwanted injury comes upon your person, Mr. Wild," I said with a playful smile. *What am I doing? I cannot behave in such a way. There is no point to winning him.*

"Indeed. It would be most welcome." His smile fluttered my stomach.

"I understand you live quite near to the renowned Stonehenge." I steadied my voice and shifted my feet, feeling the ache in my lower leg.

"Ah, that I do. Our estate sits just so—"

"It is your estate, Ben. Not ours," Daisy interposed.

"You live there, too," he argued.

"Yes, but it does not belong to me," she insisted.

"As I was saying, it sits just so that if you were to remove the great amount of dirt one calls a hill you could see Stonehenge from my chamber window."

I tried to prevent the smile that formed upon my lips, but I could not. "I wonder what one might find under that great amount of dirt once removed. Something morbid, I hope."

He laughed. I cursed inwardly. If he were not my friend's brother, I would have slighted him already. The handsome ones must be dismissed at once. He could not find me charming.

"And you have completed your Grand Tour recently, I understand?" I continued, striving to sound only moderately interested.

"Yes, I only just returned Saturday last," he replied, his smile turning wistful.

"I would be delighted to hear of your adventures," I heard myself say. *Why? Why would I be delighted? Yes, I would love to hear what the world has to offer outside of England, but I cannot risk spending more time with this intriguing man! Impossible!*

"And I would be delighted to share them with you, Miss Wakefield." His eyes brightened.

Curses!

I smiled weakly and turned away, my eyes falling upon my sister, hurrying toward us. The worry in her eyes shot unease through me. *Oh, boil and blast! Oh, what has Mother done this time?* My sister gripped my arm tightly and opened her mouth to speak. To keep her from sharing family woes, I interrupted her. "Ella, may I introduce you to Mr. Benjamin Wild, Daisy's brother."

She glanced up at him and curtsied.

"Mr. Wild, my sister, Miss Ella Wakefield."

He bowed just as the dinner bell sounded. Behind him my mother hurried toward me, Mr. Waterman at her heels. "Aurora, you are to be escorted in to dinner by Mr. Waterman!" she gasped, giving me a hard look.

I pressed my lips together and allowed the man to escort me into the dining room. Whatever his words to me tonight, my answer would begin with an *n* and end with an *o*.

Chapter Two

Ben

Daisy leaned in from her chair beside me. "Well, what do you make of her?"

"Who?" I asked, taking a bite of the duck upon my plate.

"The lady you study so intently," she said impatiently, nudging me in the side. "I see you watching Aurora. What do you make of her?"

"She is delightful," I said after a pause.

"Yes, but what do you make of her *attitude*, her lack of *zeal*, have you any thoughts on what may have changed her so?" she continued.

I raised my eyebrows in question. "My dear sister, I hardly know the lady. I cannot possibly have established her character with so little acquaintance."

She pursed her lips and seemed about to continue, but the gentleman on her right said something to distract her. *Thank the heavens.*

I took up my watch again from across the room. Miss Wakefield never once spoke first and only replied when her mother shot her a most deliberate warning look. She ate as genteely as anyone I'd seen, but rarely raised her eyes from her plate. Mr. Waterman paid her a great deal of attention. His eyes lingered on her far too much for even my comfort. By the end of the meal, I disliked the man as much as I was sure the lady did.

Miss Wakefield indeed held a mystery about her. I knew not what it was, but I wished to discover it if possible. If allowed.

The ladies among the group soon left the men to enjoy our port and lively conversation. The only conversation I felt drawn to was one that involved Mr. Waterman. I had to discover what kind of a man he claimed to be and who he really was. I soon learned that he had once been married and his wife had passed on at a young age, leaving him no children.

Mr. Sanford tipped his glass to Mr. Waterman. "A dreadful thing to lose a wife so young. My condolences."

"Indeed. And the chit left me with no heir," harrumphed Mr. Waterman, his voice slurred. "She failed at the only thing women are meant to do in life. Ruddy waste of time, she was. Still, 'tis better she's gone. I mean to make sure the next one is better behaved."

I stood, slack jawed and fist clenched. Thankfully, the men stood to join the ladies in the drawing room at that moment, or I might have said some things that would likely have resulted in our never being invited back.

My eyes scanned the room and caught a flash of green at the edge of the doorway. When I spotted Daisy and Aurora's younger sister watching the door, I had to assume that Aurora had just exited. I crossed to Daisy and sat beside her.

Daisy patted Ella Wakefield's hand. "What has you in such a fit state, Ella?"

It was then that I noticed Ella Wakefield did indeed appear upset. She glanced across the room to where her mother sat, then shifted so

To Win a Heart

her back was to her. "It is my mother. I'm afraid she has made such wretched plans for Aurora that I cannot . . ." she held her stomach and closed her eyes.

"What is it?" Daisy's voice shook with concern.

"You must help me solve this. You know Aurora has refused to marry, and my mother has threatened to force her hand. I fear she . . . I overheard her tell Mr. Waterman that he is to find himself alone with Aurora. And he is to . . . make it so she . . . Oh, the ruin!"

Daisy and I both gasped. My blood boiled.

"Isn't there anything you can do to stop her—or him?" Daisy asked.

"Papa is not in town and Mother is determined to see her married before the Season is over."

"Where is your sister now?" I asked.

"Most likely retired to the library. She goes there each evening when the men join the party after dinner. Mother knows that and is sure to send Mr. Waterman there soon."

"Where is your library?" I asked Miss Wakefield.

"Across the hall," she nodded at the doorway beside us.

"We must convince her to leave the library as quickly as we can," Daisy proclaimed.

"I have already tried to warn her, but I could not give her the reason why. Mother would punish me awfully if she found out I intervened. I know if my sister understood what Mother intends to accomplish, she would run from the house and I would never see her again. She would never speak to our mother again, and therefore I would not be permitted to see my sister again." She sniffed. "If Mother does not accomplish it tonight, it will happen on another night. I don't know what I shall do if I may never see my sister again."

I passed her a handkerchief. "Perhaps you might persuade her, Daisy."

She nodded and left the room. Miss Wakefield and I remained, awkwardly attempting conversation so as not to rouse her mother's suspicion. After a time, Daisy returned, wringing her handkerchief with a wary look upon her face.

She shook her head. "She will not come. I tried to hint that Mr. Waterman has intentions to propose to her this night, but she insists she will refuse him and he won't bother her again."

Ella Wakefield gave a small gasp, her attention following her mother, who at that very moment was crossing the room to Mr. Waterman. "She is to send him now," her voice squeaked.

My mind whirled with frantic thoughts in the few seconds it took to decide. I felt I simply must save Miss Wakefield, somehow. I could forcefully remove her from the room. I could call out "Fire!" as a sure diversion. But in any case, this scenario was sure to repeat itself until Miss Wakefield's mother was successful. Making up my mind, I slipped from the room, crossed the hall into the library, and closed the door behind me. As I crossed the room to where she sat upon a settee facing the windows, I removed my jacket and untied my cravat. Her back was turned to me, sitting sideways with one foot up on the settee, the other hung off the end. A book lay open in her hands. "Miss Wakefield. I must ask quickly, for we have little time . . ." Oh, lud. I must do this, "Will you be my wife?"

She looked momentarily taken aback, then she laughed. "No, indeed! How absurd!"

It was the answer I had expected, and now to the part I did not wish to play, and would certainly never have undertaken were it not for the dire circumstance in which Miss Wakefield now found herself. I followed through by first taking her book and tossing it to the table. She gasped in indignation but made no move to flee. I swiftly lowered to my knee, bending over her, then pressed my lips to hers. One hand slid behind her neck and the other around her waist. She pushed against me and screamed into my lips as I laid upon her. I moved my lips to kiss from a different angle. I had not done this before and I did not know if I did the thing properly, but I continued the effort and found . . . that . . . I enjoyed it. Very much indeed.

* * *

Aurora

Try as I might I could not budge the man who laid upon me. My screams were muffled against his lips. I took a breath and at the same time, his lips shifted, kissing me more gently. Another scream did not come. Instead, I closed my eyes. My arms relaxed. Tingling sensations ran through my body, giving me pleasure I had not known existed. I'd never known that kissing could be so divine as this. His lips shifted again as his head turned in another direction. I found myself returning his kisses, each one sending heat through me. My hands moved up around his neck and into his thick hair. I held him to me, my body shaking with new and confusing affections.

"Aurora!"

Mother's call brought me out of the cloud that had consumed me. Mr. Wild broke the kiss as if dazed, only half realizing someone called out. He still held me and we both looked at my mother, Mr. Waterman, Daisy, and Ella, who had all entered the room and were staring with mixed shock and confusion upon their faces.

"Mr. Wild!" Mother's tone was upset, but a hint of satisfaction hung in the corner of her eyes like a vulture. At that moment, I knew she had me. I would not escape from this unscathed. This is what she wanted. "What is the meaning of this?"

I moved to sit taller, but bumped heads with Mr. Wild. "Ow!" I cried out and rubbed my forehead. He held his nose and winced.

"Ben! You weren't—" Daisy began, but Mother spoke over her, facing Mr. Waterman.

"Mr. Waterman. If you would please give my daughter and me a moment to speak with Mr. Wild alone, it would be most appreciated."

The hardness in his eyes could not be missed. "Of course, Mrs. Wakefield." He turned and left the room. Without any regard for my person, Mr. Wild's arms circled my waist and he lifted me into a standing position. I pushed his arm away and steadied myself on my feet.

"Ella, please take Daisy to the drawing room and show her the new piano piece you have practiced," Mother commanded without looking away from Mr. Wild and myself.

"Yes, mother." Ella took hold of Daisy's arm, but not before Daisy shot her brother an infuriated look.

Yes, Daisy. I feel your sentiment exactly.

"Explain yourself, Mr. Wild." Mother raised her head and studied him as if seeing him for the first time.

Mr. Wild stood straighter. "Your daughter has captivated me, and I find myself bound by her charms."

"So much so that you could not contain yourself as a gentleman?"

He cleared his throat. "So it would seem," he answered.

"Mother. I had nothing to do with this. *He* came upon *me*." My body shook with such anger I had to tuck my hands under my arms to prevent them from coming free of my limbs.

"You did not seem to be protesting, my dear." She looked at me with raised brows. "In fact, you seemed to have been enjoying it well enough. You two are aware of what this means, are you not?"

"I am prepared to accept the responsibility, Mrs. Wakefield." From the corner of my eyes, I could see him looking at me, but I kept my face turned toward Mother.

"Are you?" Mother replied. "What will that be, then?"

"I will arrange a marriage license to be procured as soon as possible."

At his words, I spun around and dropped to the settee with my head in my hands.

"I understand you have recently inherited an estate in Salisbury?" Mother asked from behind me.

"More than a year ago, yes," he answered. "It is a worthy estate for your daughter. It brings in nearly nine thousand a year. She will be happy there."

Her eyes went large for a brief moment, but just as quickly recovered. "Very good. I am glad to hear you are at least gentlemanly enough to take upon you the consequences of your reprehensible actions."

"I always shall."

She blinked rapidly and smiled, waving to the door. "Shall we make your engagement known to our guests, then?"

I stood, a bit clumsily, but I did not care if I looked half inebriated. "Mother!"

"In order not to taint this further, an understanding must be made known as soon as possible," she said with a stern glare. "Otherwise, your reputation will suffer more than it already has."

Mr. Wild placed his hand at my back to guide me, but I pushed him away with my elbow.

Mother's eyes hardened. "You must make it believable, my dear. Even if you do not wish for it."

I lifted my chin and glared back at her. Mr. Wild held his arm out to me. Without so much as a glance in his direction, I took his arm and let him lead me from the room.

My stomach churned with anger, embarrassment, and misery as the announcement was made. The looks on some faces indicated that word had spread of our tête-à-tête. I was sure I had Mr. Waterman to thank for that. My reputation was tainted. I was stuck.

Chapter Three

Ben

The moment the carriage jerked forward, Daisy opened her mouth to speak. I cut her off. "I know what you are going to say, Daisy."

"How could you!" Had it been lighter in the carriage, I might have seen steam shooting out her ears like a boiling kettle. "We meant to save her from this, not force her hand into exactly the situation she vowed against!"

My shoulders dropped. "Do you think I wished for this? I hadn't the time to think things through."

"When do you ever think things through?" she said with a great sigh. "Ben, I love you, but you make a muddle of everything."

"I do not!"

She folded her arms and huffed. "Remember the bridge you built over the river and convinced dear Suzy to cross?"

She had to bring that up again? This was sure to be the longest carriage ride of my life if she were going to spend it listing all my childhood mishaps. I fought the urge to plug my ears. She might thump me if I did. Best to give her my full attention.

"She nearly drowned. And most recently, the street urchin you hired as a scullery maid—"

"How was I supposed to know she'd turn to thievery?"

Daisy tilted her head in disbelief. "Have you dismissed her?"

"Well, no, I . . ." I hesitated. "I thought I might give her a second chance."

She groaned. "Ben, you are proving my point. You don't think things through—even when your intentions are good. I know you wanted to help Aurora, but you could simply have joined her in the library until Mr. Waterman left!" She waved her hands in frustration.

"Yes, I could have, but what then? There would only be another day in another library where neither you nor I would be there to save her."

"But why choose this for yourself? You are now forced to wed someone you hardly know." She pressed her fingers to her temples. "I know you both, and neither of you will be happy if you do not marry for love."

"As I said," I took a steadying breath to calm my emotions, "I did not wish for this, but there is now nothing to be done but for me to marry her."

"She will despise you for this. That is certain." Daisy sat back and folded her arms in disgust.

My body felt weakened at the idea of Miss Wakefield's contempt directed at me, for I felt quite the opposite. I liked her very much. But I had felt her immediate dislike in those first few moments following our long, passionate kiss. And I felt it again when all the guests had left Wakefield's home and the pretenses were dropped. Without a glance or a word, she had pushed my arm from around her and left the foyer.

I rubbed my hand over my jaw. How would a marriage survive on such inauspicious beginnings?

My mind turned to the kiss we'd shared. I hadn't expected to feel what I felt in the library. I hadn't expected a pull deep in my soul. And if I were being honest, I had felt that tug the very first time my gaze first rested upon her. If things had turned out differently, if I hadn't behaved abominably, would something more favorable have naturally taken its course? Would love have grown between us?

Could love still grow between us?

A resolve settled in my soul. For the sake of our marriage and her happiness, I must induce love to bloom. I would do everything in my power to be the perfect husband.

***

Aurora

Mother burst into my room the next morning and hurried to the curtains to open them. She knew I hated the shock of the morning sun in my eyes. Yet she still woke me so rudely each day. It wasn't that I was against sunlight in the mornings. It was the abruptness of it that made me pull the blankets up over my head and clench my teeth.

"Wake, child. You must make yourself ready."

"No."

She huffed and shuffled closer. "You have nearly slept the day away! Mr. Wild will be here soon to take you for a ride through Hyde Park."

"He will be disappointed when he rides alone, then," I responded from under the covers.

"Stubborn child. You must go." She pulled the covers off, as I had expected, but not without a fight.

I yanked the blanket back and wrapped it around me.

She slapped my posterior and I yelped and jumped, bumping my head against the bed frame. She tugged the blanket again, this time making headway. "You must go. It will be best to show yourselves in public as much as possible to prove that your engagement is irreproachable."

"It isn't."

"Whether it is or not, you must go."

"You will not force my hand," I said with a growl.

"Your reputation is not the only one to consider." Her voice rose further. "Do you not see that your sister could be ruined by your selfish actions?"

The truth of this hit me hard in the chest. I pressed my eyes shut, wishing the whole world would stop fighting against me. I sat up and brushed my hair back. "Leave. I'll be ready shortly."

"Would you like any help—"

"No. Just go."

Her voice softened. "You used to be so kind and joyful, dearest. What's happened to us?"

Tears threatened to fall. She knew too well what had happened, and I did not wish to bring up the subject. Not wanting an audience for my humiliating preparations for the day, I shooed her from my room with a softer command for her to leave. Of course, she chose the clothing I had to wear, not wanting me to cause a scene by wearing something unfit, as I had planned. I only wished to look plain and unbecoming so it might change Mr. Wild's mind. Mother wouldn't allow it.

Mr. Wild arrived on time and with a grand smile that I did not return. Had I not been so entirely angry with him, I might have weakened in the knees at the sight of that dashing smile. As it was, I only wished to use my knees to cause him pain.

"Good morning to you, Miss Wakefield." He reached for my hand to kiss it, but I moved it behind my back.

"Aurora." Mother's warning tone brought my hand back. Mr. Wild kissed it and smiled once again.

"Mr. Wild. As you are now engaged, it would be best to address her as Aurora, and she should call you Benjamin," Mother said.

"Ben would be my preference," he answered her, but his attention remained on me.

I waved at the door. "Shall we get this over with then, *Benjamin*?" Perhaps I was a little too saucy, but my anger had dictated nearly everything I'd done of late. Why stop now?

His smile wavered, but he kept his expression light and held his arm out to me. I took it and walked with him out of the house. My abigail followed us as our escort. His steps faltered as he attempted to match my slower pace.

My confidence plummeted the moment I stood beside the carriage. I had not expected the gig to be so high. There was no step but the rail that ran from under the carriage to the horse. Mr. Wild waited patiently as I stood there wondering how I ought to proceed, or even if I could proceed. My abigail experienced no trouble at all climbing up onto the short seat behind.

"Allow me, Aurora." His voice so close to my ear startled me. His hands at my waist took all my attention, and without much ado he lifted me to the gig floor. My breath caught and I swallowed my heart back down. I shifted in the seat to the far end, where I would not touch him.

He stepped up and settled in the open carriage seat. When he sat beside me, so close we touched, I realized my mistake. I should have sat closer in the beginning, so that *after* he sat down I had room to move away. Instead I had trapped myself with no room to move when he slid in close.

"Do you often have opportunities to ride through Hyde Park?" he asked.

I did not reply. The silence stretched for a moment before he tried again.

"There are a great many paths we might choose from. Do you have a preference?"

I turned my head from him so that my bonnet kept me hidden.

The silence held. He sighed. "My horse's name is Horatio."

Hamlet. He must be a Shakespeare enthusiast.

"I named him Horatio because all the other characters die but him. And because I wish my horse to outlive the rest, that is the name I chose."

I pressed my lips together, trying not to smile.

"Of course, now that I think on it, Horatio would be quite lonely amongst all the dead. And I would not wish loneliness upon my horse either. Perhaps I was too hasty in giving him the name?"

I bit my lip and lowered my head. *Blast the man! He means to undo me with humor.* I lifted my chin and let the resentment settle back in. *He shall not break me.*

He sighed again. "Instead of speaking of silly things, what I should be doing is apologizing to you, Aurora."

I glanced at him and quickly turned away when I saw his eyes studying me.

"I should not have kissed you as I did—not that I did not enjoy it. You managed that well enough on your end." I could feel his eyes upon me.

Heat rushed to my face. The feeling of his lips on mine entered my thoughts without invitation. My body responded with a flutter of anticipation, but I squelched the memory back down.

"I say that as if I know of what I speak. You see, that was my first time kissing a lady."

Impossible. He is a rake and a flirt.

"That is, if you don't count the time I kissed my neighbor's cheek when we were only twelve. I really wouldn't count that. Especially since she propelled me into a rose bush afterward."

Of that I do not doubt. I took a deep breath in to hold onto my resentment and not let the giggle escape.

He chuckled. "It pained me to sit for days afterward."

I dipped my head when my smile broke free. *Blast you, Mr. Wild!*

I was saved when a couple known to my parents drove near. They hailed us and we stopped. I made introductions and smiled, not wishing my anger to be directed toward anyone other than him to whom it was due. I found it mildly irritating that Mr. Wild conversed easily, covering a wide range of topics in a short amount of time. We waved our goodbyes and continued on.

"Nice couple. Have you known them long?" he asked.

I didn't answer.

"Aurora," he sighed, "I truly am regretful for forcing this upon us. Had I . . ." he paused long enough that I chanced a glance at him. His brows were pulled together and he looked less confident. He took my hand in his. "I am terribly sorry."

I pulled my hand away.

"I understand your anger toward me. I do. But I hope one day you might at least speak to me. How are we to know anything about each other if we do not converse?"

"Why don't you ask Daisy?" I answered, speaking *to* him for the first time.

"It is not the same as hearing it from your own lips, dear Aurora."

Indignation flared in my chest, bubbling up to my lips. "Do not call me *dear* Aurora. I am not *dear* to you, nor are you *dear* to me."

Another couple rode up and stopped parallel to us. It took a few deep breaths to calm my anger. My dear friend Elizabeth, whom I had met during my first Season in London, one to whom I wrote often, clapped her hands in delight upon recognizing me. I dug deep and smiled. "Dear Elizabeth! How good to see you."

"Aurora. How glad I am to see you, for I have heard the strangest rumors surrounding you, and I have hope you may put it to rights." Elizabeth leaned forward in the open carriage she shared with her mother and brother.

I ignored her comment and gestured to Mr. Wild beside me. "This is Mr. Benjamin Wild. Benjamin, this is Mrs. Seward, her son Mr. Seward, and Miss Elizabeth Seward."

Elizabeth's eyes widened. She did not miss my use of his given name. Everyone said their greetings and nodded.

Mrs. Seward leaned forward. "And how are you two acquainted?"

I swallowed hard and spoke the words I dreaded. "We are to wed." I forced a smile for good measure.

Mr. Wild took my hand in his, brought it to his lips, and kissed it. He looked down at me adoringly. *Traitorous villain! How dare he look at me as if he is delighted by the idea.*

Two can play at this game. I smiled in return and leaned into him. He bested me by wrapping his arm around me. I resisted the urge to push him away and instead turned back to speak to the Sewards, who looked all their curiosity. No doubt this played right into the rumors they had heard. They offered their congratulations generously enough, and I accepted them with all politeness, promising Elizabeth she might call upon me in a day or two.

Before Mr. Wild could shake the horse's reins to urge him forward, a call came from behind. An unfamiliar man rode into view beside us. Mr. Wild cried out a joyful greeting and leaned across to shake hands with him. It was his turn to make the introductions, and I waited with bated breath, not knowing what to expect.

"Eugene, might I make known to you the dearest beauty," he pulled me closer and touched my chin with his gloved finger, "who has gone and stolen my heart, Miss Aurora Wakefield. Aurora, this ruffian is Eugene Garnet, Lord of Chessington Manor, Earl of the Sunken Wastes and Stench of the West." Both men laughed good-heartedly as though it were a common joke between them. "We attended Oxford together."

Mr. Wild! Oh, the devil of a man! I smiled at Lord Chessington. "It is an honor to meet you, my lord."

"Dear lady, it is my honor. From this declaration am I to assume there will be wedding bells in the near future?"

"There will. And you are certain *not* to receive an invitation," Mr. Wild drawled in his most important tone, as though he were above an Earl.

The Earl laughed and slapped his knee. "Does Miss Wakefield have a sister, by chance?"

"I do. This is her first Season," I answered.

"Then I shall beg you for an invitation to the wedding, Benjamin. If her sister is half as pretty as your bride to be, I shall beseech you for an acquaintance."

"You flatter me, sir, but my sister is by far the fairer of us two." I knew my cheeks must be red. I could see why these two men were friends. They both flirted shamelessly.

"I think you and your sister could pass as twins. You look so much alike, only her hair is darker in color," Mr. Wild said to me.

"And her eyes are brown, not blue," I added.

"I had not noticed her eyes," Mr. Wild said, leaning forward to add in a low voice, "Only your striking blue eyes have caught my eye, my dear."

I swallowed hard. How dangerously close he was to toying too much with my heart. I could never win his admiration. Not fully. And I could not give him mine. His words could only be empty. As empty as I felt. Empty as only this life would hand me.

Chapter Four

Ben

The clacking sound of the horse's hooves slowed. I pulled the reins to a stop one last time in front of Wakefield House. Each time we were alone, Aurora remained silent. I could count on one hand the sentences she had spoken to me outside of introductions. The outing had not been encouraging, to say the least.

I secured the brake and jumped down from my seat. Standing on the opposite side, I raised my hand to assist. She hesitated. I smiled warmly at her. "I shall not bite," I paused, then added, "unless you wish me to."

She glared at me. *'Pon rep!* Even when angry she looked attractive. She placed her hand in mine, and I felt that exercise of my heart once again. She shifted and stepped gingerly with her left foot. I could sense her unease, so I reached for her, took her by the waist, and swung her to the ground. A small squeak escaped her lips as she held her bonnet in place with one hand and her other rested on my shoulder. She wobbled for a moment and I dared not let go until she felt steady. If she never steadied herself, I would not have minded in the least, if only to be near her.

She stepped away, almost as if she gave me a gentle shove. I held my arm out for her and walked with her through the door which the butler held open. Her mother rushed toward us. "Oh, you are back! Did you enjoy your outing?"

Aurora did not answer, so I spoke up. "The weather held perfectly and there were a great many people to be acquainted with on both sides." I wished to add that Aurora's company had been pleasant and rewarding, but I could not form the lie on my tongue.

Mrs. Wakefield must have understood, for she pursed her lips. Aurora removed her hat and gloves and made to leave, but was stopped by her mother. "Aurora. Do you not wish to thank Mr. Wild for his company?"

She turned to face me. She curtsied and spoke softly. "I had a grand ride with you, Benjamin. I thank you for the outing."

"It was a heavenly pleasure to spend the time with you, my dear." I took her bare hand in mine and kissed it, now able to feel the warmth and softness with my lips. She took a deep breath and briefly closed her eyes. When she opened them, tears hovered in her lashes. *Tears?* What had I done to hurt her further?

She pulled her hand from mine and hurried away. I noticed a limp in her walk and wondered if she had been hurt somehow when I helped her down from the gig. Had I been too hasty or rough with her?

"I would like to invite you—that is to say—the Wells, our dear friends, have invited us to dine, and they have graciously extended the invitation to you and your sister," Mrs. Wakefield spoke to me, but glanced often at Aurora as she walked away down the hall.

"I would be glad of the opportunity to spend more time with your family, Mrs. Wakefield. Shall I come by the house and ride with you? Or I can bring my own carriage about, if you wish."

"Is it a nice carriage? Well sprung?"

"'Tis that. And only recently purchased."

Her smile grew. "How grand. That will do if you are willing."

"Of course. There shall be plenty of room for us all."

"Jolly good of you. Perhaps if you could spare a moment to go over some scheduling of events. I imagine you'll be attending all of our gatherings now that you two are engaged."

"Yes. Well. I am afraid I do not have the time at the moment. I must speak with my solicitor on matters pertaining to the wedding."

"Ah. We must not keep you, then. Perhaps you might come by tomorrow for tea?"

"Yes, I thank you. That will do well."

She stepped closer, her voice lowered. "Did the outing truly go well?"

"I am not one to tell a lie, so I shall spare us both and not do so."

Her lips pressed into a hard line, and I felt a sudden twinge of misgiving. "I shall make sure she behaves better in future, Mr. Wild."

* * *

Aurora

Ella ran her hand over my hair, brushing it back from my face. She kissed my head. I shifted further into her embrace and sniffed, holding a handkerchief to my nose. My shoulders shook. She shushed me and kissed my head again. "Please don't cry anymore, dearest. I hate to see your heart hurting."

My eyes studied the floral pattern on the fabric that hung around my bed frame, and I thought about how quickly my life had changed. And would change still more in the days to come.

"It could be worse, you know," Ella said softly.

"How could it possibly be worse?" I said through my shaky sobs.

"You could have been smothered in wretched kisses from Mr. Waterman and forced into matrimony with him instead."

I made a noise of disgust.

"Then you would be forced to endure his horrid breath for the rest of your days," she added.

I shook my head against her chest. "The rest of *his* days. He is much older than I and would meet his maker far sooner."

"Unless you died from breathing his foul breath."

My cries turned to laughter. "You may be right about that."

"Think on this . . . you are getting married to a gentleman and will be well cared for. *And,*" she paused for emphasis, "your husband is handsome enough that you may look at him without flinching."

I groaned. "I didn't want to be married at all, Ella."

She scoffed. "I don't believe that for a moment."

I lifted my head to look at her. "How many times do I have to try to convince you?"

"Until you're blue in the face."

I returned my head to her chest and wiped my nose.

"From what Daisy has said about her brother, I think you have found a good catch," she continued.

I huffed. "Good catches don't go around kissing women clean out of their senses and forcing them into marriage."

"Perhaps he was so smitten by you that he could not contain himself."

"Those are nearly the same words he used when asked by Mother why he behaved the way he did, but I have serious doubts about his sincerity."

"Why do you doubt?"

"We had spoken no more than five minutes with each other. There were no other interactions other than through Daisy retelling childhood stories. I do not know the man."

"And did you get to know him whilst on your outing today?"

I opened my mouth to answer, then stopped. Truthfully, no. I did not give him the opportunity. Nor did I wish to. *Let us be strangers until our dying days. He is a scoundrel to the highest degree.*

"You didn't speak to him, did you?"

I didn't answer. Evidently silence was my newfound talent.

"This won't get better if you are sour to him."

"You sound more like a mother should than our own mother. But I do not agree with you. He's a terrible man to have done what he did."

"I don't think you hated it *that* much."

I shoved away from her and sat taller. "How can you say that?"

She held up her hands in defense. "You returned the kisses and the embrace. It didn't look so terrible to me."

I narrowed my eyes. "You are on his side?"

"I am on no one's side, dearest sister. I am simply trying to make things better for you."

"I need to get ready for the dinner party. You should go."

"Don't be that way, Aurora. I'm only stating what I saw."

"Well, what you saw was a mind befuddled and . . . it could have happened to anybody. It does not mean I enjoyed it. And I will have you know I shall not wish for it again."

"Me thinketh you shall singeth a different tune once you are wed," she sang with a wicked grin.

I threw a pillow at her. She threw one back. It began. It had been more than a year since I'd joined in a roaring pillow fight with my sister. I felt an overwhelming need to at least pretend like I could beat someone senseless and part with some of the distress I felt.

Ella got in a few good blows, but judging by the way my pillow broke open and spilled its feathery contents about the room, I proclaimed myself the winner.

"Heavens! What are you two doing?" Mother's shriek stopped us short.

"She started it," Ella pointed at me. I rolled my eyes. She tried to stifle a laugh, but it broke free. I joined in.

"We haven't the time for this nonsense. We have a dinner to attend." She stepped forward and ripped what was left of the pillow from my hands. She picked the feathers from my hair and prattled on about the importance of good behavior and well-groomed ladies. I shifted off the bed and winced at the pain in my leg. Mother pulled the bell cord and fretted over the state of my room. Ella hurried away to dress, while I was stuck with Mother's constant rebukes, which moved on to how abominable I'd behaved during my ride in Hyde Park.

Again, she chose the dress I was to wear and instructed my abigail on how to arrange my hair. "Tomorrow, first thing, we will go to the millinery to be fitted for your wedding gown and perhaps buy a few new gowns. We want to keep Mr. Wild interested and not run him off."

"It will not be my gowns that run him off, Mother," I said and looked at my feet.

"Yes, I know. But if we keep him distracted enough by your better qualities, there will be a greater chance that he won't run."

Her words stung, as they always did.

* * *

Ben

A knock sounded at the door. I called out for Daisy to enter, for I knew it would be her. My valet brushed at the coat I'd just donned. From the mirror, I watched Daisy step into my room. "You look handsome, Ben. You remind me of Papa."

"That is quite a compliment, and I thank you." I smiled at her, although my heart ached at the thought of my father.

"I miss him." Her voice was soft, as if lost in memories.

"As do I. He was the greatest of men."

"He taught you well. You are just as kind," she added. "Before we attend your first ball as an engaged couple, I wanted to know your thoughts on the dinner last night."

I stiffened. Disastrous was too strong a word, yet not far off. The Wells had been the perfect hosts. The company they'd invited proved delightful. The number of people had been enough that attention toward Aurora and I did not prove overwhelming. Yet, Aurora spoke only five words to me: *You look well this evening.* That was all.

Oh, and, *Good night.*

I sighed, knowing Daisy would wait until dawn broke for an answer. "I do not know what to think of it."

"Have you tried to engage her in conversation?"

I lifted my arms and let them drop to my sides in defeat. "You were there."

"I was. She didn't answer your first few questions and it seemed you gave up after that."

I turned and headed toward the door, knowing Daisy would follow. "Do you blame me?"

"No. I do not. She is being stubborn. It is one of her failings, but she is hurting and if you could show her more compassion and talk to her more, she might open up."

"I've tried the one-sided conversations and I'm not for it." We made it to the stairs, and I held my arm out for Daisy.

We descended the stairs, pausing at the bottom to don our coats, gloves, and hats. As soon as we were in the carriage bound for the Wakefields', Daisy started up the conversation again. "Do you have a plan to break her out of her dreariness and win her heart?"

"If I did, you'd be the first to know."

"She's a romantic, Ben. I've seen your writing. Put some of that talent to good use in the real world."

I kept silent, taking a page from Aurora's lesson book. We arrived at the Wakefield estate to less than favorable greetings. Mrs. Wakefield looked in a state near to fits, though she tried to hide it behind unnatural smiles and flattering words. Ella apologized repeatedly under her breath each chance she had. Worst of all, Aurora refused to receive us.

It wasn't until Daisy ventured to go in after her that we made any progress. The moment Aurora entered the room, her beauty took my breath away. I smiled and closed the space between us. I bent over her hand and kissed it, something I would never tire of. "You look enchanting, my dear."

"Thank you." Her voice sounded strained, and as she stepped further into the light, I saw the redness around her eyes. "You . . . you look . . . well."

I offered her my elbow and led the way out the door. The carriage ride through town held little promise for the evening. Mrs. Wakefield spoke enough for us all. I found myself wishing to sit beside Aurora so I might comfort her. Something had gone amiss before we arrived, and Aurora seemed to be the target of her mother's underhanded remarks.

Aurora remained silent, her eyes fixed on the buildings and people we passed.

We entered Almack's ballroom with tickets in hand, then crossed to an open grouping of chairs at the side. Aurora wasted no time in claiming a seat of her own. I stood at her side, letting Daisy and Ella have their chance for a sit. Happily, Mrs. Wakefield found friends to converse with and left our group. I noticed that at her departure, Aurora's demeanor relaxed.

I bent to whisper in her ear. "Aurora, would you do me the honor of standing up with me on the next set?"

She looked at me. I sensed a great amount of pain hidden in her eyes. "I do not . . . That is . . . I thank you, but I do not wish to dance this evening."

"Is it your partner you object to, or dancing in general?" I held my breath and waited for her to answer.

"I would refuse anyone, so do not take it to heart. I simply am not equal to dancing as of yet."

I took the hand that rested on her knee. She did not pull away as she would have done if we were alone. "Is it too forward of me to ask why?"

She paused and drew a breath.

"Benny boy! I hoped I might see you tonight," Eugene slapped me on the back and grinned.

I nodded at him, my eyes still on Aurora. "Good to see you again." I turned to the ladies beside me. "Daisy, Aurora, you remember Lord Chessington?"

"I do," they both said in unison.

"May I present Aurora's sister, Miss Ella Wakefield. Miss Wakefield, Eugene Garnet, Lord of Chessington Manor, Earl of Chortley."

"I thought it was Earl of the Sunken Wastes and Stench of the West," Aurora said, with a tilt of a smile.

Her smart remark caught me off guard, though Eugene laughed enough for both of us. "You had better hold tight to this one or someone might steal her away." He nudged my shoulder with his. "Why is it that you are keeping all the most beautiful ladies to yourself, dear friend? I have traversed this ballroom filled with eligible ladies, at great peril to myself, my title, and my bachelorhood, in order to search out the reason for your dastardly behavior." He lifted his hand with a flourish and winked at my companions.

"Perhaps it is to prevent their being tainted by you and your unearthly stench," I replied dryly.

"Someone so dashing could not possibly smell as you describe, Mr. Wild," Ella interjected, dimpling up at Eugene, her brown eyes dancing. "And I would be careful how you toss about your words with the last name of *Wild*."

To Win a Heart

I laughed along with everyone else. Outside of her mother's presence, Ella showed promise.

"I say! I like her already," Eugene bent before Ella, taking her hand in his. "Would you stand up with me at the next set?"

"I would be delighted," she agreed.

Another gentleman came to claim Daisy's hand and soon we were left to ourselves. I took the seat beside Aurora.

"You needn't sit out simply because I choose not to stand up with you."

I leaned in. The smell of something sweet filled my senses. I breathed deeply. "I prefer to spend all my time with you."

Her blue eyes narrowed.

I squeezed her hand. "I'm not much of a dancer myself."

"Are you only saying that to make me feel better?"

"No."

She turned her attention back to the dancers before us.

"You do not believe me?"

"I find it difficult to know when someone is being true or false."

"I know I have done you the greatest of disservices, my dear. I mean to make amends."

"Nothing you can say or do will change anything."

Her words felt like claws against my soul. Digging and tearing.

The rest of the evening we sat in silence, watching the joyful celebration of the dance move around us.

Chapter Five

Aurora

Daisy blinked in surprise. "What do you mean you're not holding an engagement ball?"

I glanced at Mr. Wild before answering her. "I'm not holding a ball. I'm holding an engagement *musical*."

"Sounds perfect to me," Mr. Wild said, raising his teacup to her and then lifting it to his lips.

"Hush, you," Daisy shot her brother a look. "People don't have engagement *musicals*. They have engagement *balls*."

"I realize that, but I'm not one for dancing and I do not wish to put myself through such needless torture. Besides, it's all settled for next week, two days before the wedding."

"That's a bit quick."

"Yes, we couldn't fit it in anywhere else, so there it is," I said.

"It's hard to believe my brother and my best friend will be married in one week!" Daisy squealed. I stiffened and sipped my tea. "What is on the agenda for today?" she continued.

"We've been invited to Lord Chessington's box at the theater," Mr. Wild answered.

"Oh, truly?" Daisy clapped her hands. "I suspect that must have something to do with your sister," she added, looking sideways at me.

"I say! Do you not think me worthy of an invitation simply by merit of being his friend?" Mr. Wild objected in mock offense.

I ignored him and answered Daisy. "I suspect the same." I poured a second cup of tea for Mr. Wild and returned to my own.

"Does your mother plan to join us?" Mr. Wild asked.

I paused, my teacup frozen for a moment before my lips. "No. She is to stay at home," I answered without meeting his gaze.

"Aurora!" Ella hurried into the room. "I need you to come upstairs. I am in need of your opinion."

"Can it not wait?" I gestured at our guests.

"Oh, I am sorry," she lamented, "but I do not know which gown to wear tonight."

I took a breath, suppressing the urge to roll my eyes. "Did Mother not decide for you?"

Ella paced the room. "No. She never gives her opinion."

I flinched. Why did she dictate every detail of my life and care so little for my sister's?

"I shall help!" Daisy stood and they left together, arm in arm. I listened as Ella praised Daisy for her kindness all the way out of the room and up the stairs. My eyes turned to Mr. Wild and my heart quickened. All thoughts of Mother vanished from my mind. This was the first time we had been alone together since that fateful night.

As if he sensed my heart pounding and wished to dismantle it completely, he moved to the spot beside me on the settee. He touched the long curl that hung at the side of my face. "What is it about your sister's comment that has upset you?"

I looked at him with consternation. "What do you mean?"

"You seemed surprised that your mother does not choose her gowns for her."

I searched his eyes. "I don't . . . My mother dictates everything I do, everywhere I go, what I wear—" I paused. "I should not have said that. Forgive me. It is very good of Mother to take such an interest in me." I turned away, my face still.

He took my hand. "Aurora, we are to be married soon. We are to become one. Your burdens I will bear upon my shoulders so I might lighten your load."

"And if my burdens offend you?" My words were little more than a whisper. "What then?"

"What burden could you carry that would offend me?"

I thought back on the hurtful words I'd spoken to him thus far. Guilt tore at me. This man had only tried to make peace since . . . "I fear I have already offended you more than . . ." The words stuck in my throat. He had forced me into marriage. He deserved to feel discomfort to equal my own.

He brought my hand up to brush his lips against my bare knuckles as he spoke. "Words can be very painful. And I believe those who use harsh words to hurt others are indeed hurting themselves." He turned his eyes to me. My heartbeat sounded loud in my ears and my head felt light at his touch. "What is hurting you, my dear?" he asked.

All the pain, all the unkindness directed my way, all the despair I'd felt over the last year came crashing down on me. Tears spilled from my eyes and my chin trembled. In an instant, Mr. Wild wrapped his arms around me. I pushed him away, standing shakily and hurrying from the room.

* * *

Ben

To say the Earl of Chessington was delighted to see Ella Wakefield would be grossly understating the matter. Nor did she hesitate to share with him her smiles and blushes. I came to understand that both Wakefield sisters had a talent for endearing blushes upon their cheeks. The older of the two withheld her blushes far too often for my liking. If only I could coax her from her melancholy. I was certain she could be a delight to everyone she encountered. I'd seen bits of it shine through—her humor, kindness, and understanding.

The Earl had invited Mr. Haines to join us, a gentleman I'd met on several occasions and who I knew to be a fine fellow with a promising prospect. Eugene and Ella sat at the front of the box while Aurora, Mr. Haines, Daisy, and I sat at the back. I watched Daisy for any clues that she might be uncomfortable with the arrangement. At the beginning of the act, she seemed her shy self, but Mr. Haines soon coaxed that out of her. Both of the other couples whispered enough to fill a book throughout the evening.

I had no such luck with Aurora.

The first act ended and champagne was shared whilst acquaintances stopped by to divulge what gossip could be had, at which point I took the opportunity to hold Aurora's hand, knowing full well that if she refused with the eyes of society upon us, it would put us in an unfavorable light.

The second act began and we resumed our places. Again, I took Aurora's hand in mine while she was distracted. She tried to pull away, but I held firm.

"Mr. Wild, I kindly ask that you release my hand." she whispered, her attention set on the stage below.

I leaned in, so that my cheek touched her hair. "There are many eyes on this box, Aurora, most of whom have wagers on whether or not our marriage will indeed transpire. A whisper in an ear, a kiss," I brought her hand to my lips and kissed her knuckles, "to the hand, and a touch," with my opposite hand I ran my finger along her jaw, "upon the fair lady's skin would go a long way toward preserving our reputations and convincing the vultures we are happy with this union." With each action, my heart quickened. I thought about the kiss we'd shared. My attraction to her had not lessened, even though she had shown no encouragement. I watched the way her neck moved when she swallowed and enjoyed the curve of her cheek.

"It would only be a falsity," her soft whisper cracked at the end.

"Not on my part."

Her breathing came quicker. "You lie." Her words came out through clenched teeth, her eyes remaining forward.

I lowered our hands and let go, though I stayed close enough to whisper. "You shall find in time, my dear, how utterly opposed to lying I am."

"You cannot honestly think I believe you have any regard for me." Her head turned to me, her eyes full of hurt and anger. "For I have shown you no such esteem . . . and shall not."

"I do not know why you push me away, Aurora. Is it trust you lack? Do you not believe I am in earnest to make you happy? You have been the very dearest of friends to my beloved sister. She has spoken so well of you, and I know that young lady is still within you. And I shall not rest until I seek her out and win her heart."

* * *

Aurora

I dropped into bed after removing my burdensome garments and attachments. The instant my abigail left my chamber, I screamed into my pillow and shook with the cries I'd been holding in all evening. "How dare he!"

Why must he torture me? Why must he be so kind now, after he had been so cruel as to force my life into misery? Did he honestly expect me to fall willingly in love with him after what he had done simply because he was gentle with his affection?

"Cruel, cruel devil of a man!"

I hated his beautiful smile and dancing eyes. I hated his flirting and joyful demeanor. I hated his gentleness and kind words. I hated him.

I woke the next morning after my rage-filled cries and felt drained. Yet I did not have the choice to remain in bed. Mother insisted I accompany her on a day of shopping to try on my new slippers for the wedding and purchase a number of other accessories. The gowns we had ordered would be delivered in a day or two, but other odds and ends needed attending to.

Mary did well preparing me for the day, and before very long I'd broken my fast and stood at the ready in the entryway. From within the house, I heard Mother ranting to someone about some dislike or another. The front bell rang and Gibbs walked past in great state to answer it. When I heard Mr. Wild's voice, I felt satisfaction in knowing his time with me this morning would be short.

Mr. Wild bowed, sweeping his hat low across his front. "Good morning, my dear."

Daisy followed him in and hugged me. "Your bonnet is lovely."

"*You* look lovely," I responded.

"Oh! Good!" Mother called as she hurried in from the stairway. "You're here and on time." Ella followed behind.

I glared at Mother. When she got closer, I lowered my voice so that only she could hear. "Why have you invited him?"

"Be kind, Aurora."

Ella stepped closer. I pulled her aside. "Are you not going shopping with us?"

"No. Mother has forbidden it."

I groaned. Mother's wrath would be centered upon me, it seemed.

To Win a Heart

But perhaps my fiancé's presence would subdue her in public. One could hope.

The four of us settled into the carriage and made our way to Cavendish Square. I fretted inwardly about the idea of Mr. Wild accompanying us into the shops. The very idea! Oh, why had he agreed to come with us? It was abominable.

***

Ben

I understood the need for an escort for fair ladies shopping on the streets of London, but the invitation for me to join should never have been given. There would have been far less discomfort for Aurora had I stayed behind. Oh, had they only wished to stop in the linens and drapers shop, or a hat maker's shop, perhaps. Instead, the modesty shop, it seemed, must be their first destination.

My own footman handed the ladies down onto the pavement. I followed at a distance, trying not to overhear Aurora's worried conversation with her mother. Her embarrassment was made evident in the rose of her cheeks and the red of her ears. At last, I took her elbow and leaned in. "I do not wish to cause you discomfort, fair Aurora. I shall wait outside."

She narrowed her eyes. "Yet discomfort is *all* you have given me," she replied, entering the shop.

Another blow. Although I knew her verbal jousts came from pain that burned deep within, it did not lessen the dart to my heart. Her words tumbled over and over in my mind as I waited outside. How was I ever to make right this mess I had created?

Some time later, the three women exited the shop. Their chatter broke up the woeful thoughts within me. "Any other location you desire to shop?" I asked.

Mrs. Wakefield nodded eagerly. "We have an order of slippers for Aurora that should be fitted."

Aurora's gasp drew my attention. She looked mortified and anxious. She sidled up beside her mother and spoke in low, rushed tones. Mrs. Wakefield's lips tightened, and she shook her head.

"But Mother—" Aurora's voice broke.

The poor girl had gone through enough.

"Where is this shoe shop?" I inquired.

Mrs. Wakefield motioned to the right. "Just around the corner."

"We shall walk if you are willing, and then I shall take myself off to do my own bit of shopping whilst you have your fitting, Aurora."

"You see. It is all arranged. There's no need to get yourself worked up, child." Mrs. Wakefield smiled brightly, placing her goods in the carriage. I took Aurora's hand and laid it on my arm, then called up to my groomsman to follow us with the carriage.

Daisy linked arms with Aurora and Mrs. Wakefield walked ahead of us, leading the way. Halfway up the street, Daisy pulled Aurora from my arm. "Oh, look!" she cried out, pointing to the window of a jeweler's shop. "Look how dainty that necklace is."

Aurora, seeming to have recovered from her embarrassment, stood beside her admiring the workmanship. I stepped up next to her and placed my hand at her back, looking for any opportunity to offer kindness and affection. She didn't shy away or glare at me. Instead she pointed at a delicate chain holding an intricate flower set with an emerald stone. Her eyes brightened like a child admiring a candy jar. "That one is lovely."

"Do you like emeralds, Aurora?"

Her childlike spirit disappeared in an instant. "I do," she said, turning away. She walked on, following behind her mother.

"Be patient with her, Ben. I can see that she's hurting," Daisy murmured, taking my arm.

"Not only that, but she is furious with *me*," I sighed. "I have destroyed her future. Her happiness."

"She might see it that way now, but she will soon see how kind and gentle you are. I think once she is alone with you, and away from her mother, things will improve."

"I hope you are correct on that count."

Mrs. Wakefield stopped at the door of the shoemaker. Aurora shot me a warning look, so with a bow, I took my leave. Daisy decided to join me, leaving mother and daughter to their fitting. We backtracked a few doors down and entered the jeweler's shop.

After I judged enough time had passed for the fitting, we made our way back to the shoemaker's, where we found Mrs. Wakefield standing outside in close conversation with another couple, speaking in low tones and wringing her hands. The three of them looked about with concern etched upon their features. "Oh! Mr. Wild. Make haste! Aurora has disappeared!"

I quickened my pace. "Whatever do you mean?"

Mrs. Wakefield waved her hands in despair. "She was beside me a moment ago. But she has vanished!"

My heart sank. She wouldn't have run away due to an unwanted marriage, would she? "What direction would she have gone?"

"That is the only way that makes sense," the gentleman said, pointing to the left.

I left the group, running as quickly as I could down the crowded street, dodging street carts and shoppers. At a T in the road, I heard shouts. I turned toward the noise and spotted in an alleyway a man cornering Aurora.

Chapter Six

Aurora

"You stay away from her. She is not yours to own," I said, blocking his view of the young girl behind me. I brandished the piece of wood I'd found upon the cobblestone alleyway. It wasn't much of a weapon, and he seemed to agree with me by the way he sneered as if he had the upper hand.

"Yer a temptin' armful, ye are. Two for one, then? You'll do well with them *light skirts*." He chuckled and stepped closer.

My heart raced and my body shook in fear, but I could not yield. This child depended on me. "You shall not have her," I repeated, trying to stand firm upon my feet.

A man leapt between us, causing a gasp to escape from my lips. "Aurora!"

"Ben!"

He waved toward the end of the alleyway. "Take the child and go back to your mother."

I clung to the back of his coat. "What about you?"

"I'll see to my own. Go ahead."

I reached behind me and pulled the girl to her feet. She wasn't much shorter than I. Her terror matched my own as we took our first step along the alley wall.

"You've cost me another one, *bloke*," the man said as eased along. *Another one?*

"Then I should be knighted for a job well done," Ben responded saucily.

"You owe me."

Ben shook his head. "No, I do not believe so."

A man who appeared to be a shopkeeper ventured into the alley toward us. His eyes scanned the scene before him, then he waved me forward urgently. "Hurry, miss. 'Tis no place for a lady."

I nodded, glancing back to see Ben poised, ready for a fight. *Ben!* My fear for his well-being increased. I did not like the man, but I did not wish him harm. Especially since he'd come to our rescue.

A second man joined the shopkeeper and the two of them stood beside Ben, fists at the ready. I kept the girl tucked to my side as I hurried along. When next I glanced over my shoulder, I saw the evil man exiting the alley from the opposite side. The three men followed him out. I relaxed and waited for Ben to catch up. His eyes locked with mine and he quickened his pace to reach me.

"What happened?"

"He chose to bow out seeing that he was outnumbered." He stopped mere inches from me. One hand rested under my elbow and the other he cupped against my cheek. It was strange that his touch brought me comfort. I let out my breath and looked into his eyes studying my own with so much concern. "Are you well? Are you hurt?"

"I'm not hurt."

His hand moved down to my arm. He sighed and looked at the

child. "Are you hurt?"

"T'ain't the first time I've been in the suds, gov'nuh. She might be worse off than I," she answered and pointed at me. "Mighty shaky, she is."

"What is your name, lass?" Ben asked her.

"Ginge. Onna count o' my hair." She pointed at the fiery red hair under her cloth cap.

"Do you have a safe place to go?" I asked.

She shrugged.

I looked at Ben and held the girl's hand tighter. "I cannot leave her on the streets."

"Have you done any work as an abigail or a maid?"

She laughed. "Tare an' hounds! I ain't never been in a big house!"

"Would you be willing to learn? Do as you're told? Follow orders and the like?" Ben persisted.

"Course, gov'nuh. I'd work mighty hard iffin I had a bed to lie on and food to eat."

My heart swelled with gratitude at what he was proposing.

"You will need to learn to speak more politely," he said.

"Like you?"

He laughed and nodded. "This lovely lady who holds you so protectively is to be married to the most dastardly villain in just a few short days."

"Are ye tha' dastardly villain?" she asked.

He nodded and winked, earning a giggle. "Once married, we will travel to my home in the country, where she will need a new abigail, someone who can help her each day. Do you think you're up to that challenge?"

She saluted in response. My heart took flight. *Oh, bless this man!*

"Wonderful." He stood taller and looked over my shoulder. "My carriage is coming. It seems your mother has found us."

To Win a Heart

The ensuing minutes were a hubbub of chatter and anxious inquiries. Mother kissed my cheek and patted my hands and fussed over me, her handkerchief fluttering frequently to her eyes, until I wondered if her feelings were actually sincere. Ginge was given a seat beside the driver, and Ben handed us into the carriage. Daisy sat beside my mother, leaving the seat beside me for Ben.

"How did you end up in an alleyway with that girl?" Ben asked once we were settled on our way.

I took a deep breath to calm my shaking body. "When Mother stopped to talk to her friends, I noticed the girl walk by. I also noticed a man following her. He looked as though he had ill intentions. I feared for the child and followed to see if I could help."

"That was *very* unwise of you," Mother censured, dabbing at her eyes again. "You could have been *killed*!"

"I could not abandon the girl to her fate. I had to intercede," I asserted, my chin high.

Ben took my hand. His kind eyes brightened as he smiled at me. "I think you were very brave."

His smile took my breath away. "Thank you, Ben, for coming to our aid."

"Always, my dear."

* * *

Ben

The carriage came to a stop outside the Wakefield house. The footman handed all the women out and I followed. Mrs. Wakefield hurried in and spoke with her housekeeper. I took hold of Aurora's arm after she removed her gloves and bonnet. "Aurora, might I have a word?"

Daisy locked eyes with me, then slipped away, leaving us alone to converse.

To Win a Heart

"Which word would that be?" Aurora asked.

I chuckled and ran both my hands up her arms, then down again to hold her hands in mine. This was the first time she had let me do such a thing with no one around to observe it. Things were progressing and it gave me hope. Perhaps more than one good thing had come out of the girl's rescue. "I wish to tell you how brave you are."

"You already said that in the carriage. And that is more than one word, Ben." She almost smiled. *Oh, that she would smile fully!*

I stepped closer, my heart beating fast against my chest as I studied her beautiful face. "You are using my given name. I must confess, I like the sound of it on your lips."

She stiffened. "A mere slip of the tongue."

I lifted my hands to hold her head in my hands. My thumbs rubbed her cheeks. "Your heart is good, Aurora. I see it in you. A kind soul."

Her eyes closed tight. "What do you know of my heart?"

Heavy footsteps sounded from the corridor beside the stairway. I stepped away and lowered my hands, but not before the gentleman saw how I held her.

"Papa!" Aurora hurried to her father and threw her arms around him.

I watched with a jolt as he pushed her away, taking a large step backward. Aurora's face crumpled.

"Papa, please—"

He held up his hand to cut her off and set his hard gaze upon me. "Mr. Wild, I presume?"

I bowed. "Mr. Wakefield."

His eyes narrowed. "I assume you wish to inquire after the marriage contract?"

"Whenever it is most convenient for you, sir," I said.

"Let's get this blasted matter over with." He turned on his heel and waved for me to follow. I obeyed directly, shocked he would use such a

119

harsh word in front of a lady. "The sooner she is married off, the better."

My steps faltered. From behind me, I could hear Aurora's piteous gasp. I chanced a glance back and saw her shoulders slump, her hands covering her face.

Oh, my poor Aurora. Perhaps her father was right. The sooner I could remove her from this house, the better.

* * *

Ben

With a deep breath and a hope-filled smile, I slid the gold band upon Aurora's finger. From my youth, I had imagined this day far differently. My future wife looking up at me adoringly, hope and tenderness in her eyes, a smile upon her face. But Aurora only glanced up once, giving a weak, dutiful smile. We turned to face the crowded church and stood to be presented as husband and wife.

My hope had soared the day we rescued Ginge, only to have it dashed the very next morning by the same silent and unseen daggers she always directed at me.

I slipped my arm around her shoulders to receive congratulations from many friends and family members on both sides. Throughout the morning, I kept her close, guiding her away from her parents whenever possible. At the close of the wedding breakfast, we bade our goodbyes. Daisy and Ella took it hardest. Mrs. Wakefield cried, although the tears seemed forced and her embrace feigned. My heart broke for Aurora as she looked at her father and he turned away.

I embraced Daisy before stepping into the carriage beside my bride. "Pay close attention to Ella," I whispered to her. "Inform me if she needs removing."

With tear-filled eyes, Daisy agreed. She left that same hour from our London home to stay with friends and finish the Season. She planned to await my return in a month's time.

The eight-hour carriage ride home stretched by in silence, only speaking when stops were made for rest and refreshment. Ginge and a few other servants rode in the second carriage. The new abigail would start training and attending to Aurora as soon as we arrived at Wild House.

When the estate came into view, I had misgivings about Aurora's approval of my childhood home. Would she like it? Would she be happy here? Would she be happy anywhere? The line of trees along the path leading into the drive cast shadows. They flashed light and darkness across Aurora's face as she watched out of the window. Light or dark. Which would prevail?

With unease, I watched Aurora enter my home. I introduced her to the butler and the housekeeper who she would interact with most as mistress of the home. They stood by whilst Aurora took in the stately entry room. The Tudor-style house boasted of generations of wealth, though no title came along with it. Once there had been a title, but that was entailed off to my great uncle along with two other estates. My home had undergone a remodel during my childhood and the effect awed many.

"It's grander than I imagined," Aurora said as she turned about in the domed entry. "I didn't realize you were so well to do."

"Would it have made a difference?" I asked.

She looked at me for the first time since the wedding. She stiffened. "No."

No. She still hates me.

She moved to the stairs and I noticed she took them slowly, one at a time, a limp still hindering her. I remembered when I had first noticed it after our first carriage ride. What was the nature of this injury? I went to her side and offered my arm. She ignored me, moving to the marble banister and using it to steady herself.

Mrs. Comstock, my faithful housekeeper, followed patiently as we ascended the stairs. Ginge followed behind, whispering colorful exclamations under her breath as she looked about. Mrs. Comstock gave me a questioning look. I grinned and mouthed the words, "I'll explain later."

A moment later we passed through Aurora's private sitting room. I paused at the door to her chamber to watch her reaction upon entering her new quarters for the first time. She ran her hand along the four-post canopy bed, then turned in a circle to take it all in. Her curved figure was silhouetted by the stately windows across the room.

"Lud! Tis a lot o' room for one lass, it is," Ginge said loudly.

Mrs. Comstock pursed her lips and pointed at the two doors in the room. "This door leads to your dressing room, and this connects with the Master's chambers."

Aurora turned her head to me with wide eyes. I smiled and lowered my head. Her jaw set and she turned her back to me, beginning to speak with Mrs. Comstock.

I caught Ginge looking my way, so I waved her over. She skipped to me and stopped with her hands behind her back. "Nice place ye got, gov'nah."

I smiled and shrugged. "It's home."

"Why is it tha' the missus is so angry with ye?"

"She's not happy about this marriage. I wasn't teasing when I told you that she was marrying a villain."

Her brows rose in disbelief. "There be no villin' about ye, gov."

"She thinks so."

"Why she think tha'?"

"I made her marry me."

Her brows pulled together. "Wha' ye do tha' for?"

"To save her from an even worse villain. Two, in fact."

Mrs. Comstock moved to the door, ending our conversation.

"Take good care of my bride," I told Ginge. She saluted and turned away. Two footmen entered to deposit Aurora's trunks. I had one last glimpse of Aurora before the door closed between us. The image of her dropping her head in her hands as she sat in a chair by the fire tore at my heart.

Chapter Seven

Aurora

I clung to the girl's boney shoulders and plead with my eyes. "Promise me. You must swear you'll never speak a word of it to anyone—especially Mr. Wild."

"Lud, he don't know either?" Ginge exclaimed.

I shook my head. "Please. Promise."

She nodded. "I give ye me word." She looked down at my leg. "Does it hur' much?"

"Every day," I answered.

"He's a good'n and I'll wager he'll be understandin'."

"He's not going to know and that's the end of it."

She nodded once.

I instructed Ginge in every way proper to help me undress, how to unpack, where I preferred my belongings, and other odds and ends. It took us the better part of two hours.

"The masta said he made ye get leg-shackled an' tha' he did it to save ye."

It took me a moment to understand her meaning of marriage. When the understanding dawned, my head shot up to look at her as she folded the clothes into a cabinet. "To save me?"

She nodded. "To save ye."

"Save me from whom?"

"Didn' say. Only said from two people."

My parents? I thought about his behavior from the moment we were married. He seemed to keep to my side rather possessively. It had bothered me at first, but once I found he was directing me away from my parents' attention, I saw it for what it was. He had even stood between my mother and me and changed the subject when her criticism grew too severe.

He had been kind when we rode from London, giving me his handkerchief when he noticed the tears I desperately tried to hide. "You are allowed to cry, darling. I won't think any less of you," he had said from across the carriage. He allowed me space and quiet time. He didn't make me say a word, but let me keep to myself. I both appreciated and detested him for it.

If my life had been different, he would have been the sort of man I would swoon over. The kind I would seek out in hopes of a dance. The kind I'd like to tease in order to be rewarded with one of his winning, heart-melting smiles. I had married a devastatingly handsome, tender, and caring villain.

And I wanted to hate him. He'd changed everything.

* * *

Ben

A week had gone by without a single glimpse of Aurora. She must have spoken with a member of my staff, for she seemed to know my schedule well enough to avoid me. Each morning while I saw to the tenants or checked on the workings of the estate, my valet said she emerged from her bedchamber long enough to play the piano or search out a book in the library. Each meal she took in her room, and when my closest neighbor came to call on us, she claimed a headache and couldn't be disturbed. Every evening before retiring for the night, I knocked on the door separating our rooms and waited for an answer. Only twice did she respond. I was only permitted to give her verbal well-wishes through the door.

Things had to change.

The usual hour for my daily outing struck, but instead of in the saddle, I made myself comfortable in a high-backed chair in the library. In speaking with a maid, I deduced that she would need another book soon. My efforts paid off when I heard the sound of soft footsteps entering the room. I peeked around the chair and watched her climb two rungs up the rolling ladder, her back to me. I crossed the room and stood directly behind her.

"What is it you're looking for?"

She gasped, then screeched when her balance failed her and she tipped dangerously to the side of the ladder. Instantly I regretted my actions. I reached around her waist and pulled her off the step. I had no intention of holding her in my arms when I entered the room and made my plan to see her. Yet now I found my arms around her, holding her against my chest and feeling the rapid rise and fall of her breath. The euphoria I felt lasted only a moment before she shoved my arms away and moved at a dizzying speed away into the corner.

"My apologies for frightening you. That was not my intention."

"Then what, pray tell, *was* your intention?"

"Honestly?"

She nodded.

"I missed you and wished to speak with you. Simply to hear your voice and see you, if only for—" My answer died on my lips as she walked past and hurried out of the room. My heart sank further into the leather chair than did my body as I sat with my head in my hands. "What am I doing wrong, Papa? You've always taught me how to treat the fairer sex, but I must be doing it all wrong. Is my idea of romance so entirely off the mark?"

She seemed to enjoy my company that first meeting before I thoroughly kissed her upon the settee in the library. She even seemed to enjoy the kissing—up until the moment we were caught.

She hated me for trapping her into marriage. That much I knew. But to hold onto that for so long without making any effort at friendship puzzled me. Did she not wish for a happy marriage, or at least a friendly one? Throughout my life, I'd tried to create something better than what I had been given. I never wished to wallow in pity or drag out my sorrows. I'd always been determined to push through and find the light in the darkness. Would she not do the same?

I sighed heavily and stood. I did not know where my feet carried me as my mind wandered, until I stood at the door that separated our rooms. I knocked.

"What is it, Mr. Wild?" she answered.

No longer was I Ben, or even Benjamin. "I did not mean to interrupt your quest in the library," I said through the door. "I know you seek another book, and I do not wish to prevent you from your studies. So, I shall stay far from the library for the remainder of the day so you may return and seek out what you were looking for, if you so desire."

No response.

"You are welcome to any of the books, and if there are any you wish to acquire, I would be happy to order them for you."

Silence.

"There is already a list of books upon my desk in the library which I wish to add to my collection. You may add your own choices and I shall see to it."

A moment passed, then I heard a quiet, "Thank you."

I stepped from the door and lowered myself into an obliging chair nearby. What more could I do? I leaned on the writing desk and heard the familiar crunch and shift of parchment. An idea struck and hope sprang anew as I lifted my quill to paper.

* * *

Aurora

From the window of my chambers, I watched the clouds roll by. They raced across the sky at a quicker pace than yesterday's clouds, and I wondered if a storm was brewing. Directly below the window stretched the gardens edged in fine, sturdy walls of arched stone. Trees lined both sides of the stone walls, giving it the seclusion I adored. Beyond the garden stretched grass fields meandering off toward the hill where the mystical Stonehenge had resided for centuries. Dividing the fields and garden snaked a gathering of trees and thick bush where I assumed some small creek must wend its way through.

It all tempted me and mocked me.

How I longed to explore the paths and grounds of my new home. Yet I was not able to walk so far or over such uneven terrain alone.

Movement caught my eye off to the left of the garden, almost out of sight. Mr. Wild held a rifle over one shoulder and a bag in his other hand, obviously on his way back from a short hunt. He leaned his gun against a stone bench, sat, and scratched his faithful pointer behind the ears. He placed the bag of birds beside him and bowed as if in prayer. He stayed that way for a time, his hands clasped upon his lap, his hat preventing me from seeing his face.

Was he praying over the birds?

He shifted and lifted his head, his eyes directed at my window. My heart pounded and I stepped back behind the moss green curtains. I peeked and saw him wave a hand. I cursed inwardly. *He saw me watching him.*

Mrs. Comstock came to discuss our usual daily goings-on with the house. Knowing Mr. Wild had brought home birds helped me to plan the menu accordingly for the next few days. Mrs. Comstock was patient in helping me to understand the things I needed to oversee in the house and amongst the staff. It was a lot to take in.

Hours later dinner was brought up on a tray by Ginge. She had much improved in mannerism and decorum since instruction had begun, although I had to continually remind her which words were kinder on the ears and how to pronounce them. She prattled on about the servants she had befriended, and those who hadn't yet taken to her. It seemed several of the maids held some resentment over her position.

With the dinner set at my little table, I lowered myself into a chair. A sealed missive lay on the tray, my name written upon it in an unfamiliar hand.

I broke the seal and checked the signature at the bottom.

Ben? Why would he wish to write to me?

With a bit of unease, I started at the beginning.

My dearest Aurora,

I know you find fault with me, and your reasoning is sound. I do not blame you for harboring ill will toward me. Yet, my heart is heavy. I wish to assure you that I am eager to get to know you better. I have always longed to meet you, the dearest friend of my sister, who she spoke of so highly. I envied your comradeship. And I felt a connection to you the moment we met. I found you to be witty and delightful, not to speak of your beauty and charm.

With the heaviest of regrets, I fear I have ruined it all. For that, I am truly sorry. Please give me a chance to make amends. I would very much like to be your friend. After all, we have many long years before us. And I assure you, I am not all bad.

I know that I tend to make a mess of things. In an effort to help you understand me better, so that you might feel more comfortable in my company, I am baring all in sharing my secrets in a series of letters. I do this with great risk at my expense, yet I am determined for you to know me, my dear.

My only wish is for your happiness. I hope that I may give you pleasure and entertain you with tales of all my humiliating blunders. Be forewarned, for you have married a fool.

My father always said I was all good intention and catastrophe. But I hope I may correct this, my greatest mistake, for I could not bear for you to pay the price of my foolishness.

I wish you a pleasant evening and sweet dreams.

Yours always,
Ben

I held the letter to my heart as tears streamed down my cheeks. Why must he be so sweet and sincere? He was like a little boy, so eager to please. His words pulled at my heartstrings, yet I could not imagine a different path before us.

No, Ben, I am the fool. Yet I cannot help but continue to be so.

* * *

Ben

The smell of roasted meat and boiled potatoes drifted from the kitchens as I made my way toward the cook's domain. I entered the fray of rushing servants as they went about their pre-dinner duties.

The cook pointed at the tray to my right. "Her tray is there, sir."

"I thank you, Mrs. Lennon." I placed the third installment of my *mortifications of past events* upon it. "It smells divine," I said to the cook. "Would you please send a tray to my chambers this evening as well?"

"Yes, sir," she nodded to a young maid standing nearby, who swiftly produced another tray.

I thanked the women and hurried to leave them to it. Once in my own room, I removed my boots and shrugged off my coat. Hopefully, Aurora was enjoying the letters. It had been a couple of days since I had written the first, and I felt great anxiety to know what she thought of her blundering husband. *Husband. Lud! I am married.*

I waited until after my dinner tray was delivered to remove my cravat and roll up my cuffs. I tore into the hot roll and watched the drift of steam rise into the air. My tastebuds rejoiced in the first gravy-dipped bite.

A beautiful sound reached my ears from the closed door to my left. I paused, the roll held before my open mouth. It happened again. A smile spread across my face and I quickly crossed the room to press my ear against the door. Aurora's laughter rang out, and I found myself longing to burst through the door just to see her smile.

Her laughter died off, then moments later it erupted once more. She must be reading my letter. Anyone would laugh at my ridiculous childhood antics. I blushed in chagrin, yet still my heart felt lighter and hope burned brighter. What did my humiliation matter, if it brought her joy? If it brought her closer to me.

My feet guided me to my writing desk, where I took up my pen to convey my renewed hope to Daisy. A sealed letter lying beside the parchment stopped me. I mentally berated myself for forgetting this letter addressed to Aurora. It had arrived along with several others, and I had set it aside for her.

I returned to the door between our chambers and knocked.

To Win a Heart

* * *

Aurora

Dearest Aurora,

In the late spring of my ninth year upon the earth, I found myself traversing the jungles of Africa . . . alone. Of course, it was merely the tall grass along the River Avon behind my family's estate, but I'm willing to overlook that if you are. For days I pushed through the tangled grass, when I realized to my horror that a fierce beast—a lion, if you will (my neighbor's barn cat)—had taken up my tracks and scent.

I was being hunted.

In order to escape and make it successfully to the Lost Treasure of Wild, I must lower myself to the ledge of the Great Gulf—a chasm reaching the center of the earth (the river mentioned above). Being the brilliant nine-year-old I was, I thought it best to tie my rope to the top of the iron rail—or rather, in my childhood imagination, a rickety swinging bridge built by centuries-old Roman Gods (the bridge just down the way a bit).

Beware, dear Aurora, for you might think me a barbarian by the end of this letter. My surname isn't far off the mark. My apologies for forcing that name upon you.

I lowered myself over the Edge of Doom. Hand under hand I descended. Halfway down I found myself weakening. My arms shook and, try as I might, I could not climb back up (you'll recall there was a lion hunting me, so retreat wasn't an option anyway). What my little nine-year-old brain and weak arms had not anticipated was the force of the river's current upon my person.

If you are easily embarrassed, you may wish to set this letter aside.

No? All right then, on we go.

Throughout my youth, Mother always ordered my britches too

To Win a Heart

large so that I might grow into them. On that fateful day, as I lowered myself into the raging river, you may imagine my great consternation when I felt my too-large britches being stripped down to my ankles.

I laughed out loud, nearly choking on my dinner.

To tell the truth, I didn't have much on my back end to hold the britches up to begin with.

I laughed again, briefly holding the letter to my chest.

My arms ached as I clung to the rope. I looked around for a way out of my predicament. To my astonishment, young Miss Suzy Easton (yes, the very one from whom I stole a kiss and was promptly rewarded with a flight into the rose bushes) stood upon the bank of the river, watching me with overt interest.

I wiped the tears from my eyes, my sides shaking with suppressed laughter.

So shocked was I that I slipped and fell into the depths of the Great Gulf! I bobbed back up, of course, but not without a tooth through the lip. Little Suzy fainted dead away at the sight of the blood, falling into the mud and ruining her second-best dress, which I can assure you, I never heard the end of. I struggled to swim to the side and heave myself out of the frozen depths, losing my sodden britches entirely in the process. Thus I ran, naked as a jaybird, all the way home to fetch help for the irreproachable Miss Easton.
To this day, I sport a small scar upon my lower lip, which you are welcome to inspect at your leisure as proof of the veracity of this tale, dear Aurora.

Heat rushed to my ears. Part of me wished he'd leave out the flirtatious interludes, but another, louder, part of me quite enjoyed it.

A knock sounded at my door. I almost bade my visitor enter, when I realized it wasn't the door leading out onto my sitting room. I sat taller and set the letter aside. "Yes?"

"Aurora, I have a letter for you from my sister." Mr. Wild's muffled reply could be heard well enough. I had never yet opened the locked door, but now it seemed I must relent.

For days I had been anticipating a letter from anyone outside of this house and had yet to receive news from London. I hurried to the door, draping a shawl around my shoulders. I brushed at my long hair with my fingers and checked to see if my nightgown looked neat. After unlocking the door, I pulled it open and kept my right leg hidden from view.

My breath caught at the sight of Mr. Wild. My eyes took in his bare neck, strong jaw, crooked smile, and bright gray eyes. He leaned casually against the doorframe as he flicked his wrist forward with the letter pinched between his fingers. "Your letter, love."

I fought inwardly with the range of emotions and actions I wished to follow through. It had been far too long since I'd met with good conversation, a kind word, or a friendly smile from anyone outside of Ginge. Throughout my childhood daily, I'd received hugs from Ella, and at times when my father wasn't angry with me, he too would give an embrace. Mother hugged me when the day went well. I hadn't realized I'd been missing that. I felt a longing to be held in his arms.

Pushing those feelings aside, I took a deep breath and lifted my chin. "Thank you." I reached up to take the letter. Our fingers brushed against each other, and I felt my longing increase.

His smile faltered and his eyes grew sad. "Aurora. I'm terribly sorry."

"Good night, Mr. Wild."

To Win a Heart

I could see his body weaken at my use of his surname. I knew it hurt him and that is why I used it, but from the moment I saw his reaction, I wished to retreat and start again. Yet I could not.

I shut the door between us and locked it once again.

His muffled reply stopped me from stepping away. "Good night, my Aurora."

My Aurora. I closed my eyes and pressed my lips together. All my life I'd wished for someone to call me *My Aurora,* or *love,* or *sweetheart,* or any number of endearing terms. Now that I had my wish, it only caused me pain.

I pushed away from the wall and sat to finish my meal. Once through, I finished preparing for bed, then slipped under the quilts. With pillows propped up behind me and my thoughts most decidedly not on the man behind the door, I opened Daisy's letter.

Dearest Aurora,

I write to you with a debate in my heart. I do not wish to keep my news from you, yet I do not wish for it to hurt you, either.

Mr. Haines has this very day asked if he might court me. My heart soars at the idea, for he is the most amiable of gentlemen. I liked him from the first day we met.

I know this may sadden you, but I hope what I write next might unburden your heart and help you uncover some regard for my dear brother. He wishes for nothing more than your happiness, so I must beg you to give him a chance.

Please know I share this not to cause more distress, but to help you understand my brother's actions. The night he kissed you in the library, we had discovered only moments before that there was a plan in place, involving a certain Mr. Waterman in the library, to entrap you into marriage, much as you are now, though I fancy you would prefer my brother to that odious brute. Ella and I tried to prevent it by coaxing you from the room, but to no avail. Ben was terribly anxious to save you, knowing a little of the gentleman in question, and had not the time to think of a solution. He knew Mr. Waterman would be persistent in his purpose and would stop at nothing to prevail.

I need not recount my brother's reprehensible deeds, only please understand that in his haste, it was the best idea he could think of. Granted, he acts before thinking, and he always has. He is impulsive and foolish, but he is not vicious. He is not the sort to throw himself upon any woman, and I believe he despises himself for the disastrous results.

My brother is a good man, the very best of brothers, and a great friend. Please give him a chance.

With all my best wishes and love,
Daisy

Chapter Eight

Aurora

My emotions were at a standstill. I had no notion how to proceed. I had boiled all my hurt into anger to the highest degree. I disdained Ben and blamed him so much that I didn't know how to conceive of this new perspective. He had tried to save me. Granted, he went about it far differently than I would have liked. Yet he had come to my rescue.

I also knew what Daisy wasn't saying in her letter. I knew who had devised the scheme that would have ruined me. And ruined me it would have, for I would never have agreed to marry Mr. Waterman. I would rather bury myself in the bottom of the Thames than tie myself to that man for any length of time.

I joked with Ella that the cause of my aversion was his foul breath. The truth was, he frightened me. He wasn't a gentle-hearted man. I could see that from the beginning.

Did Mother know that? Did she even care what kind of man she thrust upon her daughter?

I woke early the next morning, nervous. I needed a friend, and Ben was willing enough to be that for me. Yet, opening up to him might prove disastrous. I waited for him in the breakfast room, but he never appeared. I wandered the halls, to the library, and along the terrace in the back, but I never happened upon him.

Late in the afternoon, I informed Mrs. Comstock that I would be joining Mr. Wild for dinner.

My anxiety grew as I awaited the occasion.

* * *

Ben

I entered the dining room to find it empty, with no sign of dinner being served. I went in search of Gibbs and found him in the drawing room, tending to the candles.

"Why are you lighting this room, Gibbs? And why is dinner delayed?"

He turned and without a change in demeanor, he announced, "Mrs. Wild is to join you tonight, sir."

My thoughts immediately went to my mother, before faltering onto Aurora. *She* was Mrs. Wild now. "Mrs. Wild? For dinner?"

"Your wife is to join you for dinner, sir," he repeated calmly.

Anxiety washed over me. I set my jaw. "Why was I not informed earlier?"

"My apologies. You were out, sir. Shall I see to the meal preparations, now?" I nodded and he turned briskly away, leaving me to stew.

I stalked to the mantle and looked down at myself in chagrin. If I had known my wife would be joining me tonight, I would have worn my best suit. I would have taken more care. I fumbled at my cravat, retying it as neatly as I could without the benefit of a looking glass.

Through the open doorway, I watched Aurora enter. As always, she was a vision of beauty. Our eyes locked and I saw my own nerves reflected in hers. She gave me a small smile, something I had hoped to see for days. My first instinct was to run to her and spin her about. Of course, I held back. I wasn't a total buffoon.

"Good evening, Aurora."

"And to you, Ben."

Ben! She had used my given name. Hope glimmered. I turned to Gibbs as he entered behind her. "Dinner is ready, sir."

I nodded once and smiled at Aurora, holding my hand out to her. She walked to my side and took my hand just as I'd hoped she would. Instead of arm-in-arm, we walked hand-in-hand into the dining room. I grinned down at her, feeling giddy and light-hearted. *She is finally giving me a chance!*

I drew out her chair. In doing so I had to let go of her hand and immediately felt the loss of her touch. Once I sat down beside her, however, I reached out for her hand again, hoping beyond hope that she wouldn't reject me. Shyly she took it.

My grin couldn't be helped. "Did you have a rewarding day, my dear?"

"No," she answered.

My smile faltered. "Might I ask why not?"

"I couldn't find you all day."

My heart did a jolly country dance within my chest. *She sought me out?* "My apologies. I was tending to my tenants for the majority of the day." I brushed my thumb against her knuckles, seeking more smiles, or perhaps a blush.

"Hopefully everything is in order now?"

The footmen followed Gibbs into the room carrying trays. I waited to answer until they had ladled a serving of leek soup into each of our bowls. Reluctantly, I released her hand. I took a deep breath and answered her question. "I hope so. At least for a few days."

"Good." She blew on a creamy spoonful, then tasted the soup. I watched her smile brighten her eyes. She liked it. That fact gave me some satisfaction.

"Why is that good, Aurora?"

"Then I won't have to spend my whole day wondering where you are and looking for you." She sounded hesitant, as if she were not sure she should have shared her answer.

Her answer, however, caused my hope to soar to still greater heights. "You wish to spend time with me?"

"If you don't mind. I know I've been a terror to be around, and I . . ." she lowered her hands to her lap, where she twisted her fingers around the serviette, "I'm sorry for how I've treated you, Ben."

"You called me Ben again."

"Do you approve of my calling you Ben, even after everything I have put you through? I have been so awful—"

I shifted in my seat, reaching out to touch her cheek. "I wholeheartedly approve. You may call me any number of things, as long as you speak to me. I've missed you."

She swallowed hard. "You truly have? Even though I've been a dragon?"

"You had every reason to be upset."

Her eyes filled with tears and she struggled to gain control. I turned my attention to my meal and waited for her to regain her composure, not wishing to cause her more distress. We ate our soup quietly until she asked what kind of tenants I have working on my land. We chatted through dinner about the property and the goings-on of production.

When we were through, we retired to the drawing room once again. She sat on the sofa and rested a pillow behind her. "Would you like a lap blanket?" I asked.

"Oh, yes, please. Thank you."

From the side wall compartment, well hidden within the trimming,

I found a folded blanket. When I returned from across the room, I found her eyes wandering over the decorative ceiling.

"This is a beautiful home, and I particularly like the paintings on the ceiling in here."

"You don't find the naked images off-putting?" I draped the blanket over her legs.

"No. I think they are beautiful and romantic." She moved the blanket as if to make room for me.

I hesitated, then gestured beside her. "May I?"

"Please do."

Her gaze returned to the ceiling. A smile pulled at her lips as she seemed to be thinking of something amusing. "I'm sorry your trek through Africa was so disappointing."

Warm blood rushed to my ears and neck. I couldn't hold back my embarrassed smile. "Yes. I learned my lesson. At least that time."

My heart quickened at her full smile and the amused tilt of her head. "That time? Were there others?"

"Ah, many, but you must wait for me to write them. Now that you put that to mind, I have yet to write one for this evening's edition." I went to stand, but her hand shot out and rested on my knee to stop me.

"No. Stay."

Her action caught me off guard, but I lowered myself back into the seat.

Her eyes dropped to her hand on my knee. She jerked her hand back and blushed. "Forgive me."

I smiled and took her hand, resting it between us on the sofa. "There's nothing to forgive." We were quiet for a moment, simply looking at each other. "Did you enjoy my horrific story, then?"

"It was as delightful as the one before it. Hanging upside down in the chicken coop didn't damage your brain, did it?"

I chuckled, remembering the first story I'd shared. "No. Although I did have a dreadful headache."

A soft giggle escaped her lips. "How long were you there?"

"It was so long ago I could not say. Time moves differently in childhood."

"That it does." She paused for a moment, and then, "Was poor Suzy traumatized by your descent into the deep waters? Did she ever recover? Or can she not look upon your face without turning as red as you are right now?" she laughed.

I looked away and shook my head. "Laugh if you must. I was only nine."

"I envy young Suzy."

I swallowed hard. "Why is that?"

"I think I would have liked to see you in such a state."

I raised my brows and smirked. "Really?"

She rolled her eyes. "I would have been rolling on the ground laughing at how absurd you appeared. Nothing more."

"Right. Nothing more."

It was her turn to blush and she did it beautifully. "You are a flirt, Ben. Of that I am entirely certain."

"Only with you, my dear." I brushed my fingers along her soft cheek.

She sucked in a breath and held it. A look of worry crossed her eyes. I lowered my hand to hold hers. She relaxed after a moment while I wondered why my touch caused her distress.

"If I do not retire to my chambers soon, I won't have time to write you your next letter," I said.

"You do not need to rush off on my account. I do not need a letter every night. Besides, I might fall asleep before I have the chance to read it."

The idea that she wished me to remain warmed me. "Did you enjoy Daisy's letter? I assume she gave you the good news of her courtship?"

"She did. Were you aware of it?"

"I was. Her friend's father has corresponded with me on all the goings-on of her time in London. I gave my approval for the courtship."

"You are a kind and attentive brother."

Her praise did more for me than she could know. I felt as if I could fly. My chest swelled with joy. "Coming from you, that means a great deal."

She looked momentarily surprised, but a smile grew and she squeezed my hand.

I raised her hand to my lips and kissed the back of it. "Did she have anything else to say? Any gossip to share?"

She laughed nervously. "You know Daisy's not the gossipy type." Her smile faded.

"What is it, darling?"

"She told me something . . . about the day we met."

My heart stopped. "What did she tell you?"

"She told me about a plan involving Mr. Waterman and the reason you assaulted me."

Assaulted. That was a harsh word. I pulled on my tight cravat. "She did?"

She nodded. "You gave up a lot to save me."

"You needed saving."

"And since then, you've been the perfect gentleman, while I've been an ogress."

"Please do not speak of yourself that way, my dear. You have every reason to loathe me."

"I thought I did. I was terrible to you, and I feel terrible now."

"Please do not fret. What's done is done. We shall move forward and make the best of it."

She nodded and gave a small smile. "You aren't angry with me?"

I shook my head. "No, my dear."

"You call me dear and darling a lot, but I cannot seem to understand why you would. I haven't given you any opportunity to know me or to have any reason to even *like* me. Why would anyone like me be dear to anyone as kind as you?"

"Because I can see the goodness in you. I saw it from the very beginning and I've learned about the real you from Daisy." I leaned forward to look directly into her eyes. "You are kind and good."

Her voice turned soft. "How can you know that?"

I squeezed her hand. "No one without a kind and good heart would stand up to a man twice her size to save a street urchin."

"She needed saving."

"So, you see. You and I are more alike than you know."

"I am grateful, Ben." She leaned over and kissed my cheek. "Thank you."

My breath quickened as my heart fluttered. "Anything for you, love."

Chapter Nine

Aurora

The tall clock on the mantle chimed two in the morning. I sat up from where I leaned against the sofa and stopped mid-sentence. "It's two?" I had enjoyed our conversation to such a degree that I had not realized so much time had passed. When coming down to dinner, I'd worried about what the night would bring. My wish had been that we could simply speak to each other civilly. My expectation was surpassed.

Ben sat taller as well. "As delightful as our conversation has been, perhaps we should retire."

My nervousness increased. We were a married couple. What kind of expectation did he have of me? He flirted and teased about kisses and other such attention, but did he assume I wished for it too? I couldn't give him that. I wouldn't. It would ruin everything.

I stood and folded the blanket. He held his hand out for it. "Allow me." When he crossed the room to return the blanket, I slipped from the room, eager to get ahead of him. Unfortunately, I could only traverse the stairs at a snail's pace. He caught up to me halfway up. His hand slipped into mine. My heart quickened and my mind whirled with worry.

He paused at my door and opened it. He followed me through the sitting room and into my bedchamber. I wanted to flee and hide. He could not be here with me. If he saw . . . *he* would be the one running and hiding. I couldn't let that happen.

He slipped his hand around to rest against the small of my back as he pulled me closer. "It has been a joy in your company this night, Aurora." With his other hand, he cupped the side of my head. I took hold of his wrist, ready to pull him away if needed. "Rest well, my dear." A soft kiss pressed against my forehead. I closed my eyes. The torture stung my heart. His gentle touches and affectionate words drew me in, but fear held me bound. I put my wall up and stepped away.

"Good night, Ben. Sweet dreams."

He gave me a small smile. "My dreams could only be sweet if they are of you."

I shook my head and giggled quietly. "I think you're confusing the word nightmare with dreams."

"Oh, darling. If you could only see yourself as I do."

"You do not know all of me, Ben. One day you will wish to run from me." He moved to step closer, but I moved quicker and stepped away. I held up my hand to stop him. "I bid you good night."

He sighed. "Good night, love."

When he left the room, I hurried to set my hair free from its pins. I brushed through it once, then struggled to remove my clothes. I didn't wish to rouse Ginge so late simply to unloose a few clasps, but the thing was impossible. At last I groaned in defeat, hesitating, then knocked softly on Ben's door. He answered, looking surprised, but pleased, and only wearing a long nightshirt. Heat flooded my body at the sight of him. "Sorry to bother you, but you are already awake and I did not wish to wake Ginge so late."

"How can I assist?" He stepped into my room with a wide grin and a twinkle in his eyes.

Oh, no. You shall not overpower me with your charms and dashingly handsome looks. "This is somewhat embarrassing, and I'm sorry to ask it of you . . . I simply need a few buttons undone."

His smile grew. "Turn around. I will make quick work of it."

I turned slowly. He began by smoothing my long hair carefully over my shoulder. I held my breath, my spine tingling. His warm fingers brushed against my skin with each clasp he undertook to undo. When he had finished, I felt his fingers brush my back from the top of my neck down my shoulder blade. I sucked in a breath and held it. He stepped back and his hands dropped.

"Will that be all?"

"Yes. Thank you," I answered breathlessly.

"Anytime." I heard the insinuation in his voice and my cheeks burned.

"Good night."

"Good night."

Sleep eluded me for much of the night, so that when at last I fell asleep, I did not rouse until late morning. I rang for Ginge. She bounced about with delight, chatting animatedly about how happy she was that I was now friends with the master. Her excitement had spread, it seemed to the rest of the staff. Ginge had overheard Mrs. Comstock speaking of our late-night visit as though it were the most positive event in years. Were all of Ben's staff so devoted to his happiness? I supposed it came as no surprise. He was a kind man, and generous. It made his marriage to me all the more regretful. He deserved better than I could ever give.

A knock sounded at the door just as Ginge finished with my hair. She looked at me in the looking glass as I sat before the vanity. "I'll see who it is." She went to the chamber room door and pulled it open. "It's yer nigh' in shinin' armor, ma'am."

I laughed at her description of him. "He may enter."

She left the two of us alone, which I hadn't expected. My stomach twisted into a knot. He crossed to where I sat and leaned down, resting his head at my shoulder, gazing at me in the looking glass. "You are so very lovely, Aurora. You take my breath away each time I see you."

Heat washed over me, and I could not meet his eyes.

"And you blush so beautifully."

I took a deep breath. "Did you need something, Ben?"

"I wish to invite you to ride with me."

My head snapped up. A heartache cracked at my chest. "Ride horses?"

"Yes. You have not yet ventured out to see the grounds of your new home, and I wish to show you everything."

"Ah . . ."

His fingers brushed my jaw as he smiled at me. "Please say you'll join me."

"Ben, I cannot."

"You do not wish to?"

"I wish to, but I cannot." *Oh, please don't ask why.*

"Why?"

My mind ran through any reasons I could give. "I . . . I don't have a riding habit."

"Oh," his face fell. "And you would need one."

"Yes."

"I shall order you one straightaway!" He stood and thumped his palms once on the back of my chair, as if that settled the matter.

I turned to look at him directly. "Oh, please don't. I do not wish to be a burden."

"You shall never be a burden, my love. We will keep to the gardens and the nearby grounds in the meantime. And in a few weeks' time, once we procure a habit for you, we shall enjoy a bruising ride in the country." He took my hand and pulled me to my feet. "We can easily go as far as Stonehenge if you wish."

"Stonehenge! I've always wished to see the formation for myself."

"Then you shall," he said, lightly touching his finger to my nose. "Come. We shall walk the gardens."

Walk the gardens. For so long I had wished to walk in the gardens. I could only manage such a thing by keeping to an even path or holding on to a strong and capable arm. No matter how great my fear of discovery, the urge to be out in nature won me over. I threw caution to the wind and accepted his offer.

"It is a warm, sunny spring day, so you may wish to forgo a coat, though perhaps a shawl will do you good," Ben said as he waited for me to choose a hat. I followed his suggestion and found a shawl as well.

I turned to him and smiled with nervous anticipation. "I am ready."

He stepped closer and placed his hands upon my shoulders. "When we return to London, I *insist* that you and Daisy shop until you exhaust yourselves. I would not wish my wife to want for anything."

I stepped away nervously. "You would spoil me?"

His smile caused one to pull at my own lips. "Indubitably."

I shook my head. "Spoil me and you shall regret it."

He pulled me from the room by the hand. "How so, my dear?"

"I would throw tantrums and make such demands they would run you into the ground. And once you'd realized the damage your spoiling had done, you should never be rid of me."

He laughed and pulled me closer to his side, leaning in to whisper in my ear. "Promise?"

I shoved at him with my shoulder. He tilted away and in so doing, caused my balance to suffer. I stumbled, but was righted once again when he slipped his arm around my waist. I moved away and took his hand instead.

My nervousness increased when we reached the uneven terrain

outside. Every shift in level would cause me pain.

I slowed my steps and walked with care as we discussed our favorite plants and trees. He had a great variety of green life in his garden, and I admired him all the more for finding joy in landscaping. He stopped many times to point out a significant tree or shrub which reminded him of one family member or another, or which had been planted for some special purpose. It was all very meaningful and well thought out. With every passing minute, I sensed the wall around my heart crumbling bit by bit. Near the back edge of the garden, he stopped at a swing.

"Would you like a seat, my love?"

I stepped back and clasped my hands. "Oh . . . no. I thank you."

"Are you not fond of swings?"

"Swings are for children, Ben."

"I know for a fact that my mother spent an awful lot of time on this very swing when *I* was young. If I had told her swings were meant for children, she would have thrown me in the river."

"Did she throw you in the river often, Benny?"

His smile grew and he stepped closer. He leaned in so his eyes were peering into my soul. "No one has ever called me Benny."

My smile faltered. "I'm sorry, I should not have—" his fingers on my lips stopped me.

"I rather like it. Please continue." The soft brush of his fingers weakened my knees. "And yes, my mother threw me into the river from time to time, until I grew too large to lift."

My eyes grew wide and my jaw went slack.

"What has you upended, Aurora?" he asked as he played with a lock of my hair.

"Your mother . . . She sounds wonderfully amusing."

"Yes. I had the very best of parents."

"And she threw you in the river, truly?"

His hands moved down my arms to hold my hands. "Yes. Is that such a surprise? You know I was an impish rogue."

I closed my eyes briefly, feeling his soft touch and attempting to gather my wits. "I've never heard of such a thing." I stepped back and walked again down the path. Thankfully, he followed.

"May I ask you something, Aurora?"

"You are allotted only one question per day, and you have already used it in asking if you may ask me a question. It really is a shame. You'll have to wait until tomorrow."

He laughed and kissed the side of my head. My heart fluttered. "You are a beam of sunshine on a cloudy day, my dear. I truly am enjoying my time with you."

"And I with you, Benny. Are you always so open?"

"How do you mean?" He paused to pick a flower and tucked it in my hair. I touched it, wondering what it looked like against my auburn hair.

"Well, you speak of the things in your heart so willingly."

"I take after my mother that way. I suppose my father, too. He was always honest and forthright. He taught Daisy and me to be the same."

"They sound like wonderful people. I wish I could have known them."

"They would have loved you."

I huffed. "I doubt that."

"Do not doubt, love."

My foot dropped an inch lower than expected and the abruptness of it nearly toppled me forward. Thankfully, Ben had a hold of me around my waist already. He pulled me closer with both arms around me. My heart took flight. "I'm sorry—I should have watched where I was going."

"I'm very glad you didn't." His flirtatious smile and the way his eyes dropped to look at my lips sent warning bells off in my head. I leaned back to push away from him, but he held me tight.

"Benny . . . I . . ." My head swam in confusion as he leaned so close his breath tickled my lips. "I cannot . . ."

"You cannot what?" he asked, brushing his lips lightly against mine. "We shouldn't . . ."

He pressed his lips a little harder. His hands moved down my back as he pressed me to him. Worry and desire battled within me as he shifted his head to angle his kisses differently. Our lips moved as if they belonged together. The softness of his lips unhinged me and my knees gave way. He held me tighter.

The sound of squeaky cart wheels approaching separated us. The gardener, my hero, drove past, but remained out of sight on the opposite side of a tall hedge. Ben closed his eyes, smiled, and leaned his forehead against mine. "Oh, Aurora. *My* Aurora."

Pain, regret, longing, despair, pleasure, worthlessness, and heartbreak pressed against my chest as I fought to hold it all in and keep my composure.

"When I entered the library that night I had no inclination what your kisses would do to me. From that very first time—"

"No." I wiggled out of his arms and turned to the house. "Please don't." I didn't see his face, but I heard the surprise and hurt in his voice as he followed me.

"Aurora. Did I say something wrong?"

"No."

He took me by the hand to stop me, but I kept walking. "What did I do?"

I didn't answer, only continued on. The faster I went the more noticeable my limp was, so I kept my pace slow even though I wished to run. I could never run.

"Please tell me what I did wrong, love."

"I cannot."

"Why not?"

"I simply cannot." I turned to the right at the fork in the path.

"If you wish to return to the house, it's this way." He tugged to the left. "Right will take you to the infamous river."

"Oh." I pulled my bonnet closer to hide my wet cheeks and tried to keep my voice even. "You can get to the river from your garden?"

"Just outside the wall, the river bends closer. It's where my family liked to swim."

"How nice."

"Will you tell me what I've done wrong?"

"Please don't ask me any more questions, Ben."

"I will relent if it's causing you distress." He placed my hand at his elbow and slowed the pace. "Besides, I have it on good authority that I've already used up my allotment of questions for the day."

Even with the tears streaming down my cheeks, I laughed, but only briefly. His hand came into view from the side of my bonnet. A handkerchief was presented to me. I took it and wiped my tears. "Thank you."

"For whatever I've done, I am truly sorrowful. I wish never to make you cry again."

I knew I would. Each time he kissed me, I would regret it. I yearned for him, but I could not allow things to progress any further. Our marriage was doomed. Perhaps telling him sooner would end the torture I was putting us both through. But if I did share the whole mournful tale, I would lose him all the sooner, and I could not bring myself to want that.

*　*　*

Ben

Once inside, Aurora returned to her room to write a letter in answer to Daisy. I followed her example and wrote the owed letter to Aurora, telling another of the woeful deeds of my youth. It took the better part of the day, and I found that when I had finished, it was time to dress for dinner.

From inside my room, I could hear Ginge rambling on. My valet ensured I looked presentable this time. I would not make myself a fool in that regard, at least. I waited in my room until I heard Aurora's outer door close. Then I snuck in and left the letter on the table beside her bed.

Our meal went smoothly and I complimented Aurora on her choice of menu. She beamed with pleasure, rewarding me with a blush. "Your hair looks lovely tonight," I added.

"Does it? Ginge is still learning, and I'm afraid she's a bit too forceful with the pins. My head feels much like I imagine a pincushion would when she's through."

"I am sure she will improve over time."

We moved to the drawing room and settled down in the same place as last night, with a blanket over Aurora›s lap. Part of me wished to tuck myself under the blanket with her, but I did not wish to frighten her off.

"Earlier you informed me that I have exceeded my allotment of questions for the day."

"Yes, I did." The mischievousness in her eyes encouraged me.

"Might I beg of you to allow me more? I am quite selfish, and I do wish to know you better."

She sighed heavily as though I were a chore to handle. "If you wish it."

"I wish it, sweets." I lifted her hand to my lips and kissed it below her pinky.

Her eyes followed my action and a small sigh escaped her lips. "I cannot promise I will answer."

I held her hand close to my face and asked about her favorite books and music composers. Between each question, I kissed a different part of her hand. She acted as though she enjoyed the attention, judging by the soft squeaks and sighs she issued. For a time I tiptoed around the burning question I really wished to ask, and when my curiosity could no longer wait, I rashly plunged in. "What happened to your leg to make you limp?"

She stiffened and turned her head from me. "I don't wish to talk about it."

"Does it pain you?" She didn't answer, so I persisted, "I only wish to help you if I might. Daisy mentioned you had a carriage accident over a year ago. She also mentioned you don't dance, nor are you as active as you once were. I only wish to help."

She sighed and watched her finger play with the edge of the lap blanket. "The subject brings me such pain to discuss, but in order to satisfy your curiosity, I will tell you this . . ." she took a shaky breath, "Yes. There was a carriage accident. I was injured and mostly healed. I suffer daily pain and cannot bend my ankle; therefore, I cannot dance, or mount a horse, or step up into a carriage . . ." She paused. "That is all I wish to tell you."

"Is there nothing to be done for your ankle?"

"No."

"I've always been fascinated with medical studies. May I see the injury to better under—"

"No!" She hurried to tuck her feet awkwardly under the chair. She paused to pick up the blanket that had fallen to the floor. "Forgive me, Benny. I'm . . . I should retire for the night."

I stood and took the blanket from her. "May I walk you to your room?"

She hesitated.

"I will not press you on the matter any longer. I promise."

She nodded her consent. I hurried to put the blanket away and walked with her until we both stood inside her room. I bent and kissed her lips. One soft kiss was all I was permitted before she stepped away and bid me good night.

She rang for Ginge, and I left with a heavy heart, wishing I could alleviate her troubles. Her outer door closed and all the noise ceased from her room. I stood close by the door after my valet had left. I lifted my hand to knock on her door so that I might tell her I was sorry. My hand froze at the soft sounds of her weeping. My heart made a new place of residence in my stomach. My shoulders grew heavy. *What causes her such sorrow? Why will she not lighten her burden by sharing it with me? Why does she push me away when I know she wishes me to be near and enjoys the attention?*

What am I doing wrong?

Chapter Ten

Aurora

I stretched under the blankets and peeked out from behind my bed curtains. The morning had just begun and the birds outside my window rejoiced in the new day. I sat up in bed and turned to the glass of water on my side table. My eyes landed on an envelope with my name written in Ben's hand. A smile grew in anticipation of the new story I might find.

I broke the wax seal, read his note, then paused to wipe the tears of laughter from my eyes. Already he was entertaining me with his wit and devilry. A knock sounded at my door, and assuming it was Ginge, I called her in. My eyes moved across the page, and a giggle shook my body. A moment later I felt a shift in the bed. I gasped and startled seeing Ben smiling at me.

"Forgive me. You did say to come in," he said, lifting his eyebrows.

I quickly looked him over and felt my face warm as my eyes took in the nightshirt he still wore. "I'm sorry, I thought you were Ginge."

"Do you wish me to leave?"

"Uh . . . no. You may stay." *I hope I do not regret that.*

"I see you're taking great delight in my blunders." He leaned against one arm. His dusty blond hair fell in his eyes and a hint of stubble on his jaw gave him an unkempt, rugged look. *Oh, I love to look at him.*

"I am."

"Where are you in my jolly tale?"

"Did none of your friends, nor you, ever suspect you might acquire splinters from sliding down a hollow tree trunk? Honestly. How could you not know?"

He chuckled. "It never crossed our minds. And by the time the first of us ended the long slide, it was too late and there was far too much noise coming from the river to hear anyone call up."

I laughed. "How unfortunate."

"Yes," he laughed, "and unfortunate for the doctor called to mend us."

"He must have seen far too many bare posteriors for his comfort that day."

His deep chuckle did strange things to my heart. "Indeed."

"Do all of your mishaps have to do with your backside, Benny?"

"Nearly. My adventurous spirit outweighed my intellect far too often back then. And when you added even more adventurous young boys to the mix, the sum total of our collective intelligence diminished drastically."

I laughed heartily. "Then perhaps I am to congratulate you for making it to the ripe old age of twenty-two."

"I should receive a reward, I think."

"Perhaps."

We grew silent, yet our smiles continued, studying one another's eyes. He had such beautiful gray eyes, which seemed to change their color based on the shade of his suit or the light from the windows. My mind returned to the story of his descent down the bridge when I saw the small scar under his lip. Without thought, I reached out to touch it.

He kissed my fingers. "This is your scar from the adventures into the Great Gulf?" I began to move my hand away, but he took hold of it and kissed my palm. I sighed and closed my eyes. When I opened them his nose nearly touched mine.

"You are the most beautiful woman I have ever known, my love. You have stolen my heart with your wit and charms." His lips met mine with such softness I felt my heart melt. I pressed my hand to his chest, but couldn't seem to push him away. Warm lips brushed across mine then pressed again. I returned the kiss and felt the world tilt. My eyes fluttered shut and my hand moved up his chest, brushing along his skin until it settled in his hair. He moved closer, pressing me into the pillows as he kissed me more deeply. With my heel digging into the mattress, I shifted my body higher and further into the pillows.

He responded by moving his lips along my jaw, under my chin, and down my neck. I gasped, attempting to catch my breath and steady my heart. His hand moved to my hip and up to my ribs. My eyes shot open. "No. Stop." He kept kissing, kept moving right along. I pushed against him hard enough that he sat back. "No!" I slapped him across the face.

His shocked expression broke me. I gasped at the harshness of my actions and covered my mouth in horror. The rejection in his eyes caused my own to tear up.

"I'm so very sorry," I said under my hands.

Ben lowered his head and shook it, "Forgive me, Aurora. I—I assumed too much." He abruptly stood and hurried from the room.

I dropped myself into my bed and wept. I wept for broken dreams and for what I couldn't have. I wept for the hurt I'd caused Ben. I wept for my own stupidity for allowing my heart to get involved. I wept for love lost.

* * *

To Win a Heart

Ben

With a groan of discouragement, I tossed the crumpled paper aside and dropped the quill back into its jar. I ran my hand along my newly shaven jaw. The action reminded me of the slap she had given me. More than the slap, the rejection stung. My pride had been deflated.

I'd lost the respect of the woman I most cherished. Three days had passed since. We went to church during that time. She held my arm and sat beside me in our family pew. She smiled when introduced to neighbors and spoke when I asked her questions. But once we were safely alone in the carriage again, silence reigned. She took my arm quietly as I escorted her back into the house.

That was the extent of our interactions over the past three days. She remained in her room. I did not seek her out, fearing further rejection.

I sat back and wondered how to write to her. I hadn't done so in days, and I did not wish to share more of myself if she were not interested. *Why is she so averse to getting close to me? Surely, she felt the same desire as I.* She sighed and kissed me in return. She held me as though she did not wish to let go. Her dainty hands moved across my skin and through my hair. Surely these were not the actions of someone disinterested.

I pulled another blank parchment onto the desk. I could not share something humorous. I didn't have it in me. Instead, I chose a story that brought me great shame and guilt. Something that would match how I felt now.

* * *

Aurora

To my darling Aurora,

Truly, I did not wish to offend or harm you in any way. I shall not impose upon you again.

This will not be one of my usual narratives. It will not fill you with joy and delight. For that I am sorry. Not all of my childhood misconduct was the result of innocent stupidity.

You will remember Suzy from prior childhood tales. She and I shared a great many larks, until a fateful day when her father suffered a stroke. He passed out of this life abruptly. Suzy was devastated. She was only thirteen and I fourteen. She came to me in need of comfort, and to my undying shame, I refused to give it.

I was home from school for the summer months. Two of my schoolmates came with me to spend a fortnight at my home. When Suzy happened upon us near the river, in need of compassion from me, my friends teased me for having a girl dawdling about. I laughed at her and turned her away, fearing my schoolmates' rejection more than the harm I might cause Suzy.

She went away, rejected and broken. Not many months later, while I was away at school, she tried to take her life. Thankfully, she did not succeed, but her family sent her away to live with an aunt. At the age of seventeen, she contracted a fatal fever and passed from this life into the next. I never had the chance to tell her how sorry I was. She will never know the regret I carry.

I made a vow never to turn my back on those in need. I will always assist, and I shall always try to brighten a sorrowful heart.

I fear I have failed in that respect, dear Aurora. Many times over I wish I could have found a way to save you by which you would not have been harmed by me. I cannot ask you to forgive me. I do not deserve such a gift. Please know I wish you joy.

In two days I shall return to London to assist Daisy with the particulars of her possible engagement. You will have the peace you deserve in this home of yours whilst I am away.

I wish you well and will think of you continually.

With all my love,
Ben

I pressed the letter to my heart and cried. How could I have muddled things so entirely? How could I have hurt him so thoroughly? Yet, how could I have done anything differently? I couldn't give myself to him without his seeing my mutilated limb. He couldn't see or I would lose him.

"No one will ever wish to marry her," Mother had said after the surgery. "She will be rejected by all of society."

I shook my head and wiped the tears away. He would be gone for some undisclosed amount of time. Was he truly leaving to assist Daisy? Or did he wish to flee my presence? Was I pushing him away from his home? Before my rejection of him, he had planned to take me with him and bring Daisy home. He even talked of inviting Ella and any suitor that wished to follow, as well as their families. We planned to host our first house party together.

I wished I could give him everything a woman could give. A companion he could be proud of, who would stand by his side and be a support.

But I couldn't give him that. I couldn't do this to him. I couldn't force him from his home simply because we did not get on.

Having made my decision, I folded the letter and placed it on my desk. I had to make him aware of my plan before he departed for London. I owed him that much, at least.

Chapter Eleven

Ben

Light danced across the moving current as the river ambled over the deep rocks where I stood. I threw another rock and felt the satisfaction of its disappearance into the depths. A bird called from the opposite side, as if daring me to plunge in and sink along with the stone. "That I already have, little bird."

How could my heart sink any lower?

I would leave in the morning—without my bride. Never would I have imagined traveling to London without my new wife. Now it seemed I had no choice.

The snap of a twig brought my head around. My heart quickened at the sight of Aurora walking toward me. Her eyes were fixed on the trail before her as she leaned heavily against the stone wall descending toward the river. I hurried to reach her to give her aid. She looked up in surprise, then allowed me to help her to the water's edge.

"Do you come here often?" she asked after an awkward pause.

"I come here to think."

She nodded. "I suppose I've given you much to think about."

"You might say that."

"Forgive me."

"You need not ask for my forgiveness." I picked up another rock and tossed it into the river.

We stood in silence for some time before she broke it again. "I've come to tell you that I'm going home."

I jerked my head back. "*This* is your home, Aurora." I said the words more forcibly than I meant to.

"I mean that I am returning to my parents' home."

"You're leaving me?" My voice cracked. My heart found residence in my boots.

"I do not wish to push you from your home, Benny. You belong here. I do not."

I chucked another stone into the dark water, feeling my heart sink along with it. "May I ask you something?"

"Of—of course."

"Did you enjoy it?"

"Did I enjoy what?"

"Our conversations? Our kisses? My touch?"

Her cheeks pinked.

"You did. Didn't you?"

She lifted her chin. "That has nothing to do with this."

I moved to stand directly in front of her. "Yes, it does. You enjoy talking to me. We conversed well into the night, for hours. Each time I kissed your hand, you sighed with pleasure. Each time I kissed your soft lips, you returned my passion. Do not stand there and lie to us both when I know you wished for it."

"I didn't wish for it."

"You lie!"

To Win a Heart

She held her head higher. "I didn't wish for it."

"Do you know what my mother did when I lied or was too stubborn to listen?"

"No."

"She threw me into the river." Of course, Mother knew I enjoyed that particular form of punishment, but that was beside the point.

Her eyes narrowed. "You wouldn't dare."

"Wouldn't I?" I swept her off her feet and threw her over my shoulder as easily as if she had been a sack of grain.

She screamed. "No! Ben! Put me down!" I lowered her body into a cradle position and swung my torso to the side. She screamed again as her body flew through the air and into the water. I knew the water was deep enough for her to submerge safely, and once she got her footing, she could stand with the water reaching chest level. The current was not strong here. She would be safe.

But she wasn't.

Her head didn't emerge for what seemed like eternity. Finally, I saw it bob up briefly before she sunk beneath the surface once more. I waded into the water, reaching for her, only brushing her arm before she slipped away. I pushed in further, grabbing hold of her gown. I pulled her closer, then up out of the water. At last her head broke the surface and she gasped for air.

"My leg!" She coughed and gasped again. "It's gone!"

Gone?

I lifted her into my arms and carried her up the bank, lowering her onto a patch of grass. Her body shook harder than I'd ever seen anyone shake. Her sobs tore at my heart. When I leaned away, I saw the reason for her intense distress. Where there should have been two feet, there was only one. Halfway down her shin, her leg ended in a stub.

The reasons for her limp and why she did not participate in any of the activities she had once enjoyed became clear. I turned to the river and pushed into it again, diving in to search for any sign of her wooden leg.

How could I have let this happen? *Yet another instance of my mucking things up. I am truly the stupidest of men.* Yet she had never allowed me a single glimpse of her tragedy. How was I to know?

It didn't excuse my behavior. I should never have thrown her in the water.

I searched for several minutes without finding anything. Not a shoe nor a stocking.

When I turned back to where she lay, I found the place empty. A few yards up, she struggled to crawl in her soaked clothing. Her body shook with cold and sorrow.

I stumbled out of the water and hurried to her side. She slapped my hand away when I lowered myself to help her up. "Get away from me." She didn't yell, but her tone hurt far more than if she had.

"Let me help you."

"Leave . . . me be." Her words sounded off, as if she struggled to even breathe.

"Aurora! Stop being so stubborn and let me help you!" I pulled her to her feet whether she wished it or not. "Your knees will be covered in blood by the time you reach the house." I cradled her like a babe and carried her from the river.

Her cries caught the attention of my gardener, who, upon seeing us rushing toward the house, offered his assistance. I instructed him to look for a wooden leg in the river. Although I knew it must have been washed down with the current, still I must make every attempt to find it. Upon entering the house, I called out for a bath to be made ready, and for Ginge and Mrs. Comstock to come at once. By the time I reached Aurora's room, her cries had turned to quiet weeping. I lowered her into a chair and took her head between my hands.

She turned her head away, avoiding my gaze.

"Aurora. Forgive me. Had I known, I most certainly never would have . . ."

She shifted her body away from me and I lowered my hands. She did not wish to hear my apologies, and I did not blame her for rejecting them.

Ginge entered and upon noting the missing leg, turned her worried eyes to me. "Where's 'er leg, gov?"

"You knew about this."

She nodded.

And yet her own husband did not.

"Please forgive me, Aurora." I kissed her head before I stood. "Please forgive this blundering fool." Ginge began unfastening her mistress's sodden dress, so I left the room to give her privacy. "What have I done?" I turned and fled from the house, back to the river to make what recompense I could.

* * *

Aurora

Ginge entered my room that evening with an armful of clean linens. She smiled at me and without a word, took to her task of freshening my bed. I sat in the window seat with a blanket across my legs. I turned my attention back to the world outside, looking at it with longing. Gone were the days I could run through a field, easily ride a horse, or go for a swim.

From the moment I could walk, I had spent my days outdoors, whether cold or warm, rain or sun. Most of the contention between my mother and I was due to my wild tendencies. That changed after the accident. Then our quarrels centered around my refusal ever to marry.

The hardest thing to lose was my freedom of choice. My options and how I wished to live my life were taken from me the moment the carriage fell on my leg and crushed the bones of my foot. Society demands that the fairer sex look and behave a certain way. I could not now meet that standard, to say nothing of the embarrassment and humiliation of revealing my disfigurement to a gentleman.

The memory of the horror on his face as he looked upon my leg flashed across my mind and brought about another round of tears. I had been so careful. I wore longer than usual gowns and never chose shoes that did not encase my ankle. I kept my wooden leg tucked behind the other each time I sat. Throughout the last six months after receiving my prosthetic, I practiced how to walk so that my limp was not obvious. I was so careful.

I dropped my head into my hands once again, wishing I could take back the last few months. I could have done more to refuse to attend the Season with my family. If only I had managed to get sick enough that I could not travel.

A knock sounded at the door and I jumped in surprise. Ginge crossed to the outer chamber door and opened it just enough to peer through. Then she opened it wider, and when she turned around, she was holding my prosthetic, the wood dark from the water, in her hand. *He found it!* "Tis the masta. Do ye want to see 'im?"

"No."

She turned back to the door.

My earlier plan came to mind. "Wait. Yes. I wish to speak to him."

My heart squeezed when he entered. Oh, the sight of him nearly unhinged me. He took a few steps in. "Oh, Aurora, please—"

I held up my hand and halted his steps. "Stop. Please do not . . ." I took a deep breath and continued. "Are you still planning to leave for London tomorrow?"

"I . . . well, I have not thought about it since the, ah, well . . ."

"If you decide to go, I wish to join you."

His eyes widened and he took a step closer. "You do?"

I held my hand up to stop him again. "Do not come closer. Please. I want to return to my family. I believe they are still in London, although I cannot be certain, for they do not write."

He swallowed hard and searched the floor as if trying to understand my request. "Last I heard from Daisy, they plan to remain another week or two."

"If it's not in any way inconvenient for you, I hope to return to my father's home."

He kept his eyes lowered and nodded. "If you wish it."

"Thank you." I turned back to the window.

A soft sound, as if he'd whispered, reached my ears. It almost sounded like a declaration of love, but I could not be sure, nor could I hope for such a thing. He left the room without another word.

* * *

Aurora

The groomsman handed me down from the carriage at the inn in which we would rest for an hour from our travels. Ginge followed me out, and Ben dismounted his horse. My first step toward the door gave me unease. Since the leg had dried, I found the leather straps to be far looser than before. The leg never fit perfectly, but now it slipped each time I attempted to walk. I reached down and pressed a hand against my traveling coat to adjust it once again. Ben appeared at my side, placing a steadying hand on my back.

I shot him a sideways glance of annoyance. He needn't pretend to be concerned. With a deep breath, I pushed forward into the inn. We made our way to a seat in a private parlor, where we ate our soup and roll and drank our tea. Once refreshed, we waited outside for the carriage.

"Joe, where is Mr. Wild?" I inquired of the groomsman.

"He's gone on ahead, miss."

My heavy heart grew even more so at this news, even if it was for the best. The carriage pulled to a stop in front of us. The groomsman handed me in and Ginge followed behind. The large windows inside the carriage gave me a decent view of the surrounding village. As I adjusted in my seat and placed my reticule beside me, I peeked out at the passersby. One man caught my eye, his face in shadow. He turned just as I glanced his way, but I had the feeling he had been watching me. *Have I seen him before?*

The carriage lurched forward and the man disappeared from view. We still had three hours left until we would arrive. It would be late, but at least we need not bed down at an inn. For that I was grateful.

The hours passed as I dozed fitfully in the bumpy carriage. Suddenly a great popping sound brought my head up with a snap. A man's loud, angry cry invoked fear in my heart. Ginge's wide eyes met my own. A squeak escaped my lips from another crack cutting over the horse's whines and the call of men. *Gunshots!* Through the window, I watched Joe fall to the ground at the side of the carriage. My breath froze. The carriage sped up, but only for a moment before it came to a stop.

A man in a wide hat stepped into view through the window. My heart pounded with dread. The lower portion of his face was covered by a cloth, but his hard eyes burned into mine. He opened the door and held the gun at the ready. I moved to sit in front of Ginge, blocking her from view.

"Ye thought ye could escape me, didn't ya, lady-bird," the man gloated.

"How dare you!" I gasped.

"Ye don't rememba me, do ye?" He chuckled, then pulled the cloth down to his chin.

I cringed and Ginge whimpered. *The man from the alley! He's the one I saw at the inn!* I gathered my courage and said, "Leave us be. We have nothing of value to give you."

"Course ye do." He moved closer to the door, leaning in further. "I 'ave the two of ya. Ye took me prize before, now the both of ye will make up for lost blunt."

I looked about the carriage and found no weapon or any way to free ourselves from his ill intentions. He waved his gun at us. "Now out with ya."

If only I had a gun or even a stick to beat him with. *A stick to beat him with! My leg!* I had a stick, of sorts. I reached under my dress and hurried to unlatch the buckles. His eyes followed my actions and his gun pointed at me.

"Leave the knife be."

I removed my hands and held them up, showing they were empty. "Why would a lady such as I carry a knife? I only wished to retie my stocking."

He waved with the gun again. "Out."

I shifted just enough to free my leg. It dropped to the floor of the carriage, and with one quick motion, I swept it up and pummeled him hard over the head. Over and over I hit him as hard as I was able, using the heel of my boot to do as much damage as possible and crouching low to avoid the flailing gun. He shielded his face with his arms and stumbled back, cursing.

All at once, his arms dropped and his face went slack as his body jerked forward. He toppled to the ground, unconscious, and behind him was revealed a most welcome sight. I dropped my leg and whimpered, "Ben."

He reached for me, clasping my hands and looking me over in concern. "Are you injured?" He peered at Ginge cowering behind me.

We shook our heads. "He did us no harm," I said, relief flooding my voice. My chin shook and tears filled my eyes.

"Your leg worked wonders, my dear. How very brilliant of you. And so brave." He kissed my head and then let go of my hands to retrieve a handkerchief from his pocket.

All I could do was cry and laugh. He always seemed to have a handkerchief at the ready.

"Is Joe and 'erbert dead?" Ginge asked the question I should have. In all the commotion, I did not think of our groomsman and driver.

"They are alive but wounded. I'll bring them to you, then tie up this miscreant. You two stay in the carriage and tend to their wounds. Do you have the constitution to give aid?"

I nodded and hurried to replace my leg.

After some time, Joe and Herbert occupied the space across from us. The sight of their bloody clothing at first made me lightheaded, but it soon passed, and I was able to assist. Their wounds were mostly superficial, Jo having been shot in the arm and Herbert grazed by a bullet along his side. Ginge did most of the work, tying tourniquets and binding the wounds with strips of cloth torn from our petticoats.

Ben returned to the carriage several times to check on our progress, then to inform us that he had the dastardly highwayman tied to the back of the carriage and was ready to depart in search of the local magistrate. "Are you ready?" he asked, taking in the sight of the two pale-faced men slouching across from me. I nodded and he disappeared. With my head out the window, I watched him climb into the driver's seat.

We were not far from our destination, but the men did not look well when at last we arrived. They were escorted out along with the ruffian on the back of the carriage. He, however, was not bound for the rest and care of a doctor.

Well into the dark early morning hours we finally came to a stop at Ben's home in London. He handed us both down from the carriage and I nearly crumbled.

"Are you weak, my dear?" Ben asked in my ear with me held close to his side.

"No. My leg isn't . . ." I took another step and heard a crack in the wood. The leg felt as though it were about to split in half. I felt the pinch of a crack against my skin. My heart sank. I took another step and it worsened. "I think my leg is broken."

Ben pulled me closer. "Arm around my neck, love. I'll carry you inside."

I didn't fight him off, but did as he asked. He lifted me easily and carried me all the way into my chambers. I had not seen the room before, and in the dim light of the candles, I found it fashionable and inviting. He laid me carefully on the bed.

When he straightened, I gasped, having only just gotten a good look at him. "You have blood on your person. Is it yours? Are you injured?"

"No. It must be from Joe and Herbert," he answered, looking down at himself with an appraising eye.

Ginge entered the room and stood ready to assist me.

"May I get anything for you?" He brushed his fingers through my hair and touched my cheek, studying me.

"A new leg," I laughed, even as my frustrated tears fell. *How am I to get around now?*

He shifted to my leg. "May I see the damage done? Perhaps it can be repaired."

I nodded and watched him remove the leg. He looked it over in the dim light. "Might I take this, just for a day or two?"

I nodded once again, hiding my stump from view so he would not have to look upon the eyesore.

He hastened from the room, hardly looking at me.

Chapter Twelve

Aurora

  I woke to a shift in my bed and felt soft, gentle hands touch my hair. The smell of lilacs brought to mind Ella. My eyes fluttered open and I found my sister's angelic face looking at me with sad and worried eyes. "Ella. I have missed you terribly," I said, reaching out.

  She kissed my head. "And I have worried over you excessively."

  I shoved her shoulder. "Then why did you not write?"

  Her brows pulled together. "I did write."

  We studied one another for a long moment, both of us seeming to land on the same conclusion. My interfering mother at work once again.

  "I heard what happened with the highwayman," she said at last.

  I wiggled into her arms as she lay beside me. "It was the most terrifying experience of my life."

  "Ben said you broke your leg lambasting the man over the head." The laughter in her voice brought a smile to my face.

  "That I did. It felt good."

"Well done, Aurora."

I had to ask the question, but couldn't bring myself to voice it. Ella, being Ella, knew where my thoughts had wandered.

"The news has spread." She sounded regretful. "Society will know you have only one leg. I'm sorry, love."

Now I shall be known as a cripple. They will pity me, or feel disgust at the thought of my defect.

A sob broke loose and my body shook in Ella's arms. A knock sounded at the door. Without waiting for an answer, Daisy entered, hastening across the room to perch on the edge of my bed. "Are you hurt?"

"No. I am well," I sighed.

Her eyes surveyed the blanket where a lump under the covers should have been. "Why did you not say anything, Aurora? Did you think I would scorn you, my dearest friend?"

I said nothing.

"You are my friend, and you always will be. In fact, I'm inclined to be angry with you for thinking so little of me. If you hadn't just had an abominable encounter with a hideous highwayman, I might give in to it. As it is, I forgive you," she went on, a hint of irony in her voice. She tried to hide the smile that twitched the corners of her mouth, but I saw the telltale dimple in her cheek. She slapped my leg petulantly. "And I'm a little put out that you placed Ben in the same category!"

I shifted and turned my face away, growing suddenly sober. "You did not see the look of horror on his face when—" I broke off, swallowing the lump in my throat.

"There must have been another reason for his distress. How did it happen? Tell me everything."

I took a deep breath and relayed the story.

To my surprise, she shook her head and smiled. "He did *not* look at your leg with horror, Aurora. If I know my brother, and believe me, I *do*, he was mortified by his actions and completely appalled that he had lost your limb."

I considered her words as she continued.

"He cares for you a great deal, Aurora." She took my hand firmly in hers. "Stop pushing him away."

"Did he tell you that he cares for me?"

She hesitated, then, "Not in those words, exactly, but I can see it in his eyes." She stood, smiling. "Ella, I'm glad you've come to stay with us. I look forward to our time together. I need to see to my things and get settled in. I shall see you at dinner."

"I won't be going down for dinner. I have no leg to walk on."

"Then may I request to join you in your room for the evening meal?"

I smiled and looked to Ella. "Will you join us as well?"

"Of course."

"Will you be staying here with us?" I persisted.

"Ben has invited me to return with you to Wild House. I shall stay with you until the marriage takes place, then be on my way," Ella said with a smirk.

I looked at Daisy and sat up. "You're getting married?"

"Perhaps. He hasn't asked yet, but I expect it any day."

Ella cleared her throat expectantly.

My eyes widened when I turned to her. "*You're* getting married?"

"The Earl of Chortley has asked for my hand, and I have happily agreed," she announced with a giggle.

I threw my arms around her. "Oh, love! I am so pleased!"

"He is the very best of men, and I am so happy he has chosen me." She returned the hug. "He is to join us with his family at Wild House for a time. His family lives close by, so it works out beautifully. I am quite happy."

"As am I," I said.

"As am I," Daisy added, throwing her arms around us both.

Daisy and Ella settled in, then returned when dinner was served in my chambers. We chatted about wedding plans and the events I'd missed whilst away. When I asked after Ben, both ladies admitted they hadn't seen him all day.

The next day followed much the same pattern. I very much enjoyed my visit with Daisy and Ella. We spent time reading aloud, play-acting stories and laughing at one another. But at the end of the day, I found myself feeling rather dull. I had neither seen nor heard from Ben. Daisy's declaration of his affection for me diminished in credibility as time slipped by.

I woke the next day and lay in bed wondering what I could do. In truth I did not wish to return to my parents' home. Yet, what else could I do? I shifted in bed. Something hard prevented me from moving over. I sat up and blinked in the early morning light. A long, thin package lying next to me piqued my curiosity. I sat up and pulled it into my lap with a long yawn. I opened it and found the object wrapped in cloth, a note laid neatly on top.

My darling Aurora,

I hope this letter finds you well. It took a great many hours and a great deal more effort than the carpenter wished to give, but I have at last completed it to my satisfaction. My hope is that I did not muddle the thing too terribly, as I have in so many other ways with regards to you.

Let me know if I may be of any further assistance.

With all my love,

Ben

* * *

Ben

"Ben."

The voice of an angel woke me, calling my name. A shift in the bed beside me brought me fully awake. Aurora leaned toward me on her elbow, her chin in her hand. The loose curls of her long hair framed her smiling face beautifully. I sat up and looked her over, taking in all of her beauty. She lay beside me on the bed, wearing only her night shift. "You are a deep sleeper, Ben."

"Am I?"

"Yes. Decidedly." She leaned on one arm, her shoulder pressing up to her ear. My heart fluttered at the sight of her. "I could have painted a great landscape upon your face, one worthy of the Royal Court, and you would not have awakened."

I chuckled.

Her eyes turned from playful to soft and kind, with a faint hint of sadness in their blue depths. "You made me a new leg?"

"Indeed, though not alone." I moved to study the wooden leg peeping out from under her nightgown. "Does it fit properly?"

She turned so that I might see it fully, which was unexpected. "It pinches at the buckle, but it fits far better than the last one. How ever did you manage it?"

"With a lot of help." I pointed at her leg. "May I see?"

She nodded and swung her leg closer so that it rested in my lap. Her cheeks colored and my heart hammered. She tucked her hair behind her ear and looked at me shyly. "It doesn't offend you?"

"Why would your leg give offense?" I unbuckled the strap that fastened higher above the knee. "You have a very fine leg."

She looked up at me in disbelief, "You think it's fine?"

"Very." I smiled. Her eyes shone with tears and everything became clear. "Aurora, love, did you think I would not want you because of your leg?"

She pressed her lips together and nodded. The tears spilled over and ran down her cheeks.

"I adore every part of you, my love. That's never changed, nor will it."

She smiled and wiped at her tears with the back of her hand. "Truly?"

I nodded. "Truly." I ran my finger along the side of her knee. "Is this where it pinches?"

She nodded and closed her eyes. Her breathing quickened at my touch. I smiled and brushed my fingers against her skin again. She sucked in a shuddering breath, her eyes still shut. "I do believe you're blushing, Aurora."

"Benny?" she gasped and I ran my fingers up higher on her leg, then down again.

"Yes, my love?" My fingers trailed around the end of her leg then moved up the side above her knee.

She opened her eyes to look at me. "Thank you for not letting me drift away. You have given me hope and joy. And . . . I love you."

My heart burst from its painful cage. Love entered in and filled every part of me. "And I love you, darling Aurora."

She reached up and pulled me closer. "Then show me."

"It would be my honor, love, to show you how much I adore every bit of you, inside and out."

Our lips moved together as she laid her body down and I followed. She broke free from our embrace only long enough to giggle at my touch. What a glorious sound! My wife—my Aurora—had finally broken through the strangling hold of despair and lies. This happy soul was my true Aurora. She was saved after all.

Thank you for reading!
Please help me continue to publish by leaving a review on Amazon and Goodreads and share with friends! Every little bit helps get the word out to other readers and allows me to keep sharing my stories, so thank you in advance!

Other books by Christine:

Shariton Park Series:

A Time for Shariton Park

A Season for Shariton Park

There are plenty more to come, so sign up for my newletter found on my website at www.AuthorChristineMWalter.com for the next book!

Acknowledgments

There ain't no way in h-e-double-hocky-sticks I could have published on my own. There are so many people to thank, my head is spinning. First, I'd like to thank my children and my hunk of sugar lovin' husband for giving me time and support to write. Thank you to my editors, Alexa, Lynne, Lauri, and Shelley, for the crap load of junk you had to sift through to polish my work to what it is now. If there are any mistakes, they're all on me. Sometimes, I can't see what's right in front of my face, so they are lifesavers.

A huge shout out and thanks to Katie Gardner at Sapphire Midnight Design for the beautiful cover. Thanks to my family and friends who have encouraged me in getting my stories out there. I have a big appreciation for Lynette Taylor. You were the first to push me to write, so thanks for giving me the confidence to do so. Traci Hunter Abramson, thanks for the pat on the back, the kindness, and the inspiration to keep going. Thanks to my Sweet Tooth Critique group for all your feedback. Also, my ANWA writer's group. You ladies rock!

Thanks to all the YouTubers and other authors on social media who have shared their publishing experiences and advice with the world. It's a huge support to those starting off.

About Christine M Walter

Christine adores her husband, her three adult*ish* children, and her attention-seeking dog, Chewbacca, so much that she'll pause writing and reading just for them. Well, most of the time. When she's not drawn to writing, she often spends time in Lego building, painting, drawing, hiking, rock collecting, and off-roading through saguaro cactuses near her home in Arizona. Christine's artwork has been featured in the novel *Blackmoore* by Julianne Donaldson, as well as in the movie *8 Stories*. Christine has been the recipient of multiple awards in the first chapter contests. Seeing new places and experiencing new cultures are top on her list of desires. In fact, her sense of adventure inspired her and her family to sell their home, move into a 400-square-foot RV, and travel the country simply to see and enjoy life outside of the norm. Best year ever!

You can reach Christine by following her on Instagram, TikTok, and Facebook. Also, check out her website at @AuthorChristineMWalter.com

Insta- @AuthorChristineMWalter

FB- Christine Walter Author

TikTok- @authorchristinemw

Printed in Great Britain
by Amazon

53086214R00106